A CARNIVAL OF KILLING

A CARNIVAL

OF KILLING

Glenn Ickler

NORTH STAR PRESS OF ST. CLOUD, INC.
Saint Cloud, Minnesota

ISBN 978-0-87839-584-2

First Edition: September 2012

Printed in the United States of America

Published by
North Star Press of St. Cloud, Inc.
P.O. Box 451
St. Cloud, Minnesota 56302

www.northstarpress.com

www.northstarpress.com   Facebook - North Star Press

ACKNOWLEDGMENTS

The author expresses his gratitude to the following for advice, encouragement and information that contributed to the writing of this novel:

Stephen Rogers of the New England Chapter of Mystery Writers of America; Carol Monroe of the Ramsey County Manager's Office; Ramsey County Attorney Susan Gaertner; Karen at the Crowne Plaza Hotel in St. Paul; and the Web sites for the St. Paul Winter Carnival Association, the Klondike Kates and Vulcanus Rex.

Chapter One

Body on Ice

I T'S NEVER GOOD NEWS when the phone rings before sunup.

Publishers Clearinghouse does not call at 5:46 a.m. to inform you that you're a millionaire. The IRS does not call to tell you that there's been a gigantic tax error in your favor. Your attorney does not call to say that a distant and previously unknown uncle has died and willed you a five-bedroom, beachfront home on Maui.

Who does call at that hour is my boss, City Editor Don O'Rourke of the *St. Paul Daily Dispatch*. And, as previously noted, it's never good news.

When the bedside phone rang on this particular late January morning, I groaned and tried to roll over and grab the receiver. However, Martha Todd and I had been working our way through the book *101 Positions That Lovers Will Love*, by Swami Sumi Something-or-other, and we had fallen asleep still locked in the fifty-seventh position, with my right arm pinned beneath Martha's left hip.

"You gotta roll off," I muttered, pushing against her right hip with my left hand. She mumbled something similar to "moomph," untangled her right foot from behind my knees and rolled away. I rolled the opposite way, groaned at the numbers I saw glowing on my digital clock, picked up the receiver and mumbled something similar to, "Hullo?"

Don never wasted time with such formalities as an actual greeting. Or even an identification. I think he assumed the content would point to the speaker. "The cops have a female body in a driveway on Mississippi River Boulevard," he said. "Your Siamese twin's already on the way." He gave me a house number and the nearest cross street. I said I'd be there in twenty minutes.

"Make it fifteen," Don said. "And dress warm. It's twenty-five below out and the wind chill is minus forty."

"Thanks for the warning," I said, but he'd already hung up. The temperature didn't surprise me. The St. Paul Winter Carnival had begun, and this celebration almost always ushered in the coldest twelve days of the year.

"What's happening?" Martha asked.

"A woman's body in a driveway on Mississippi River Boulevard," I said. "And the temperature is twenty-five below with a wind chill of forty below."

Martha groaned. "Call Don back and tell him you've got the flu. Then come back to bed," Martha said in a muffled voice. I turned and saw that she'd pulled the covers over her head to escape the chilly bedroom air.

"I can't do that," I said. "Al's on his way. I have to be with him."

"Would you go with Al if he jumped off a bridge?"

"He wouldn't risk breaking his camera."

I'm Warren "Mitch" Mitchell and, thanks to Al's help, I'm a reporter for the *Daily Dispatch*. Al is Alan Jeffrey, the paper's best photographer and my best friend since our college days. Ten years ago he dragged me out of a bottomless pit of alcoholism, where I'd sunk after my wife and baby died in a car crash, and hauled me to the Hazelden treatment center. When I returned to the real world, Al helped me find an Alcoholics Anonymous chapter and slide into a reporting job.

Because Al and I worked and played together frequently, Don labeled us the Siamese Twins. He said we were joined at the funny bone, which in our case was the skull.

Noting that one of my allotted fifteen minutes had already gone by, I shuffled into the bathroom, peed and brushed my teeth as rapidly as possible and examined my face in the mirror. A shadow of stubble covered the whisker-friendly areas not encompassed by my sand-brown mustache, but I decided to leave shaving for another time. I'd already used up five minutes.

"I hope the poor woman isn't nude," Martha said as I pulled on my woolen long johns. "Tell me that Don didn't say she was nude."

"Martha, the woman's dead. She can't feel the cold."

Martha, who really was nude, sat up and let the sheet slide off her breasts, a stimulating sight even in the dim light coming through the open bathroom door. "How do you know that? Have you ever been dead? Who knows what the dead can feel when it's way below zero outside? Besides, she might have been alive when he dumped her there."

"He?" I said.

"The man who killed her."

"You're sure it was a man?"

"It always is." Her voice had gone muffled again. I assumed she had submerged under the covers again.

"Thanks," I said. "I'll tell the cops." While we talked, I got into my warmest skiing combination of black stretch pants, orange wool socks, red turtleneck, blue sweater, green down jacket and yellow wool hat. I'm a regular rainbow on the slopes.

Martha popped out from under the covers again and sat up. "Oh, my God. Get out of here," she said. "You're hurting my eyes."

"I'm gone." I leaned down, kissed her lips and gave her right breast a parting pat. "Stay warm."

I grabbed my cell phone off the bedside table and stuffed it into an inside jacket pocket. On the way to the hall door, I pulled on a pair of fleece-lined après-ski boots and my heaviest leather ski gloves. As bulkily bundled as I was, the air stung my face and sucked my breath away when I stepped through the outside door. Moisture from the atmosphere had condensed, frozen into tiny crystals and fallen onto the blacktopped parking lot, coating the surface with a slick layer of ice. The effect was that of a skating rink illuminated by a streetlight at the outer edge of the lot.

Walking gingerly, I reached my three-year-old Honda Civic without falling. I had seven minutes remaining on Don's time table when the engine turned over with a complaining groan and sputtered into life. I turned the defroster on full blast, got out with my scraper and cleared a patch of windshield in front of the driver's side. The defroster would melt the rest as soon as the engine warmed up.

With every moving part in the Civic creaking from the cold, I backed out into the alley and turned toward the side street that led to Grand Avenue, a normally congested commercial-and-residential street that ran past the front of the building. As I turned west on Grand, I found it all but deserted thanks to the time and the temperature, and I coaxed the Civic up to forty miles per hour on the frost-slicked roadway. Eight minutes and three slip-sliding turns later, I was going south on Mississippi River Boulevard.

A voice on the radio was warning drivers to use extra caution because of the dangerous road conditions as I pressed the gas pedal closer to the floor. On my right, the earth dropped away to the level of the river more than a hundred feet below. I said "thank you" to the Civic for the stability of its front wheel drive and kept the pedal down.

Multiple sets of flashing red and blue lights heralded my arrival only two minutes later than Don had demanded. Half a dozen squad cars, two unmarked police cars, and an ambulance were parked at various angles on the street adjacent to the driveway. All engines were running, emitting white clouds of frozen exhaust fumes that gave an ethereal effect to the scene.

The body was sprawled near the end of the blacktopped driveway, surrounded by warmly-dressed cops, both uniformed and plain-clothed, who had tramped away most of the frost. This entourage was in turn encircled by a streak of yellow crime-scene tape that kept Al Jeffrey, three TV cameramen, and two TV reporters a good fifty feet away from the action. The presence of two red-faced, shivering uniformed cops just inside the tape discouraged any efforts to sneak a closer peek.

Al was also bundled in his heaviest winter wear, topped with a red jacket and ski cap. His dark mustache was rimmed with frost from his frozen breath.

"You look like a fire hydrant in that outfit," I said as I approached.

"I feel like a sausage in a tight casing," Al said. "I've got three layers under this jacket—sweater, turtleneck, and T-shirt."

"What about the body? Martha wants to know if she's nude."

"Why? Has she suddenly got a thing for nude women?"

"She wants the naked truth. Actually, she's afraid the poor girl is suffering."

"Judging from what I saw before the current mob scene convened, the bare facts are that the girl is neither nude nor suffering. In fact, she's wearing quite a fancy dress. But her arms are bare."

"Martha won't like that," I said.

"Why not? Americans have a Second-Amendment right to bare arms." Al's jokes weren't always stand-up comic quality, but they helped relieve the tension at sickening scenes like the one before us.

What appeared to be a five-and-a-half-foot-tall mushroom wrapped inside a brown tent-like, ground-length, fur-trimmed woolen coat with the collar turned up, topped by an oversized red knit ski hat, moved away from one of the TV cameramen and stopped in front of us. "Any idea who the victim is?" asked a voice that echoed from within the mushroom.

All I could see between the hat and fur collar was a pair of blue eyes above a dripping red nose, but I recognized the voice. Inside the bundle was Trish Valentine, a blond and buxom reporter for Channel Four.

"Haven't a clue," Al said.

"I just got here," I said. "You're up awful early aren't you, Trish?"

"This is Trish Valentine reporting live, any time of day or night," she said.

"As long as you're reporting live, you're better off than she is," Al said. He pointed to the rigid form being loaded like a log onto a gurney for the ride downtown to the morgue.

I walked up to one of the uniforms at the yellow tape and asked about the victim. He was flapping his arms to stimulate blood circulation and fend off frostbite, but he stopped long enough to tell me that the body was that of a white female about five-foot-four and "kind of pudgy." He added that any additional information would have to come from Homicide Chief Brown.

"Do you know who found her?" I asked.

"You'll have to get that from Detective Brown."

"How about the people who live here?"

"Their name?"

"Yes, their name."

"You'll have to get that from Detective Brown, too."

As I gritted my teeth and pressed my numb lips firmly together, Al spoke softly behind me. "Nice try."

Looking past my purveyor of limited information, I saw Detective Curtis Brown, chief of homicide, slide into one of the steam spewing unmarked cars. "I don't know why we're freezing our butts out here," I said. "I can call Brownie from someplace a hell of a lot warmer than this."

"How cold is it?" Trish asked. "Do you guys know?"

Before I could relay Don's weather report, Al said, "It's so cold that the flashers in Rice Park are just showing people pictures of their privates."

"How do you get to Rice Park?" asked Trish.

CHAPTER TWO

Getting Warmer

MY ARRIVAL IN THE NEWSROOM AT quarter to seven brought forth a chorus of comments from the early birds on the city and copy desks. These ranged from, "Who's that masked man?" to "Hey, Mitch, how was the skiing?"

Ignoring these lesser creatures, who had been basking in the warmth of the newsroom while I was bearing the rigors of the frigid northland, I pulled off my gloves and hat, ran a hand over the light-brown haystack of hair to push it down, smoothed my moustache and clumped over to Don O'Rourke's desk to tell him what little I knew.

"Christ, I got everything but the 'kind of pudgy' part just sitting here," Don said. "I hope your twin did better with the camera than you did with the questions."

"It's easier to shoot pix long range than it is to yell questions at people who aren't listening and don't want to answer," I said. "I'll get on the phone to Brownie and get as much as he's willing to tell me. And I'll write a description of the scene that'll raise goose bumps all over your body."

During my ten years at the *Daily Dispatch*, I have cultivated a relationship with the head of the St. Paul PD Homicide Department, Detective Curtis Brown, otherwise known as Brownie. This has not been an easy field to cultivate because of the nature of Brownie's job and his personal tendency toward minimal conversation with the media.

Brownie has a private number known only to a select few. After dumping my puffy ski jacket on the floor beside my desk, I punched in the secret digits and heard Brownie's phone ring a dozen times before he picked it up and gave his customary one-word answer: "Homicidebrown."

I always respond in kind. "*Dailydispatch*mitchell."

"Was that you I saw standing out by the tape dressed for a day on the slopes?" asked Brownie.

"It was," I said. "But I'd never go out on the slopes on a day like this."

"Good thinking. Very thoughtless of some asshole to dump out a body on a day like this."

"Do we know what the body's name is?"

"We do, but you won't until we notify the next of kin."

"How did you identify her?"

"She had a little cloth purse attached to the belt around her waist. Her driver's license and a credit card were in it."

"It looked like she was dressed kind of different," I said, hoping to elicit some details. "Not the usual winter combo of sweater and slacks."

"As you'll probably see in your partner's pictures, she was wearing a purple dress with a big skirt and very short sleeves."

"Do you think it was some kind of costume?"

"I ain't saying what I think at this time."

"Was her coat or hat anywhere around?"

"Nope. We've got guys out looking for that stuff."

"What about her underwear?" I had to ask that one.

"No comment on that at this time," he said.

I was jotting down notes but getting very little to put in a story. "How about the guy who found her? Can you identify him?"

"We're not releasing his name at this time."

"What about the owner of the house where the body was found?"

"I can't release his name at this time but you must have a city directory in your office," Brownie said.

"Well, thanks. That's a start. Any idea how long the woman had been there?"

"She was frozen stiffer than a teenager's dick on prom night, so we're guessing she was dropped there around midnight."

"Any idea when can I get her name?"

"Like I said, not until the family has been notified. I'll have Franny call you when the chief gives me the word." Franny is Frances Furness, the police department's public information officer.

"Why don't you call me?" I asked. "After all, we're friends."

"Friends?" said Brownie. "You consider us friends because your partner always takes pictures of my good side? Because you buy me a steak every other week?"

"I've never bought you a steak."

"Might be worth trying."

"Only if I can put it on my expense account," I said. "Meanwhile, what else can you tell me?"

"Nothing at this time," said Curtis Brown. "Have a good day." The line went dead before I could say thanks.

Of course we had a city directory. I thumbed through it, found the house number on Mississippi River Boulevard and discovered that the owners were John J. Robertson, Jr., and Cynthia Q. Robertson. I copied the phone number and called it. A woman answered: "Robertson residence."

"Is this Mrs. Robertson?" I asked.

"This is Mrs. Alexander, an employee of the Robertson household," she said. "Mrs. Robertson isn't taking any calls right now."

"Actually, it was Mr. Robertson I wanted to speak with," I said.

"Mr. Robertson has gone to work. You may be able to reach him there."

"And that would be where?"

She gave me a number that I recognized as the main line for the State Capitol and an extension that meant nothing to me. I thanked her, punched in the Capitol number and followed up with the extension. After several rings, a woman answered: "*Enquirer*, Liz Adams speaking."

I had reached the Capitol bureau of our Twin Cities newspaper rival, the *Minneapolis Enquirer*. "Hi, Liz," I said. "This is Mitch Mitchell at St. Paul's finest newspaper. Is John Robertson there?"

"He just went to sit in on a seven o'clock breakfast meeting in the governor's office," she said. "Can I have him call you?"

"Absolutely." I gave the *Daily Dispatch*'s number and my extension.

"Can I tell him what it's about?" she asked.

"It's about what he found in his driveway this morning," I said. It seemed so obvious that I almost prefaced my answer with, "Duh!"

"What was that?" Liz asked.

"He hasn't told you?" My voice went up an octave in incredulity.

"He came in, said he was running late and dashed off to the meeting. What hasn't he told me?"

"Check the *Daily Dispatch* website," I said. "And have a good day."

I almost ran to the city desk to tell Don that the man who found the body was an *Enquirer* reporter and that he hadn't said anything about the discovery to his colleague at the Capitol bureau. "I wonder if he bothered to tell his city desk that his driveway was the center of a crime scene," I said.

"Let's look," Don said. Both the *Daily Dispatch* and the *Enquirer* deliver printed editions of the newspaper to subscribers' doorsteps and newsstands in the morning. The print edition is augmented electronically by Website pages that are updated frequently throughout the day. Don called up the *Enquirer*'s home page and scanned it. Whereas our home page was headlining what few details we had about the Mississippi River Boulevard body discovery, the *Enquirer* was showing nothing.

"What'd you say this clown's name is?" Don asked.

"John Robertson, Jr.," I said. "And I'm aware of who that is."

"Aren't we all?" Don said. He stood and shouted across the newsroom. "Hey, everybody, want to hear a funny story about the son of the publisher of the great *Minneapolis Enquirer*?"

It was after ten o'clock when Franny Furness finally called. I set my half-full coffee cup to one side and prepared to copy the information.

"The victim's name is Lee-Ann, spelled with a hyphen and an upper-case A, Nordquist," Franny said. "She was twenty-seven years old, single, and the mother of a little girl named Sarajane, all one word no hyphen, age five. She is also survived by her parents, Leonard and Sophie Nordquist of St. Paul."

Franny gave me the parents' address, which was on the East Side where many of the city's Scandinavians are clustered. "She also has a sister, Lori-Luann, spelled with a hyphen and an upper-case L, who lives in Fargo, God help her."

"The parents seem to have a great affinity for hyphens," I said. "Anything special about Lee-Ann? The name sounds vaguely familiar."

"As a matter of fact, there is something kind of special," Franny said. "She was Klondike Kate at last year's Winter Carnival."

CHAPTER THREE

Legacy of Klondike Kate

THE ORIGINAL KLONDIKE KATE WAS A weather-hardy woman named Kathleen Rockwell, who made her way across the snow-capped Alaska mountains to the gold fields around the Yukon and Klondike rivers during the Gold Rush of 1898. The St. Paul Winter Carnival's Klondike Kate presided over a make-believe northern-frontier casino known as Klondike Kate's Cabaret.

"Do we know the cause of death?" I asked.

"It appears to be strangulation," Franny said. "But that's not official. Autopsy results should be available sometime late tomorrow."

"How about motive? Any signs of sexual assault?" That question must always be asked when a woman is murdered.

"No comment on that until after the autopsy," Franny said."

"Time of death still around midnight?" I asked.

"The body was probably dumped in the driveway about midnight. She may have been killed an hour or so before that. Again, we'll know more after the autopsy. You won't want to print this little tidbit because you're not a tabloid, but it's taking a while to get the body thawed out."

I remembered how stiff the corpse had been when it was lifted onto the gurney. "That's more than our readers need to know," I said. "Is the chief planning to make a statement, or is this all until tomorrow?"

"The chief has scheduled a briefing for all media here at the station at 1500 hours," said Franny. Great, I thought. Just in time to allow the TV evening news to tell everyone the story more than twelve hours before our printed edition subscribers would see it in the morning paper.

I thanked Franny and put down the phone just as Al found an open patch big enough to accommodate half of his butt on the corner of my desk.

"What do you know about Klondike Kate?" I asked.

"Not much," Al said. "Some of the old ones perform with the current winner at the saloon, and they all dress like 1890s Gold Rush bar floozies. Why are you asking?"

"Because our frozen dead woman was last year's Klondike Kate. I've got to get some background on the program."

"Didn't we see her a couple of weeks ago at the contest?"

"We did. Her name is Lee-Ann Nordquist."

Because I gag while watching anything resembling *American Idol*, I don't normally attend the Klondike Kate competition. However, Al's wife, Carol, knew one of the contestants, so Martha Todd and I went to the show with the Jeffreys to cheer for her.

Carol's friend had lost to a hydrant-shaped 180-pound blonde (have I mentioned that Klondike Kate is traditionally "kind of chunky"?) with a voice that could shatter storm windows all the way to the Wisconsin border. Lee-Ann had helped the new Kate, whose name was Angela Rinaldi, put on the winner's sash and joked about the need for a longer piece of satin to encompass the expanse of Angela's substantial bosom.

"I need to tell Don who the victim is," I said.

"Good luck," Al said. "You know what he's going to say."

I knew, but I walked to the city desk and told Don anyway. And, as if on cue, he replied, "Call the family. See if you can get a picture."

These were the most dreaded words a reporter could hear. Nothing in this business was more distasteful than asking for a comment and/or a photograph from the parents or siblings of a crime, accident or suicide victim. There's a fifty-fifty chance the person you contact will want to send you off to join their recently departed relative, so reporters have developed two rules: If phoning, hold the receiver at arm's length after identifying yourself. If ringing the doorbell, step back out of arm's reach before the door opens. If you don't hear a scream or feel the breeze from a punch, you've got a chance of achieving your objective.

Given my druthers, I'd go on one of those god-awful TV reality shows where contestants eat raw cockroaches soaked in snail slime or fall 200 feet into a barrel of bubbling green acid than ask a mother for a comment on her daughter's murder. But Don had given the order and, good soldier that I was, I obeyed.

A man answered the phone. "Nordquist residence."

"Mr. Nordquist?" I asked.

"I'm his next door neighbor," the man said. "Are you a reporter?"

"Yes, sir, I am," I said, and stretched the receiver away from my ear.

"Go fuck yourself," he said loud enough for me to hear and slammed down his receiver.

Satisfied with this response, I reported it to Don.

"Okay with me," Don said. "But don't do it on company time."

I was off the hook for talking with grief-stricken family members, but I still needed some quotes and a picture of Lee-Ann Nordquist. My next call went to the St. Paul Festival and Heritage Foundation, which ran the Winter Carnival. After wading through the usual routine of "press one, press two, press three," I finally got an operator who connected me with Bob Sherman, the executive director.

I phrased my request for a reaction carefully in case Bob hadn't heard that Lee-Ann Nordquist wouldn't be entertaining at the Klondike Kate Cabaret any more. Bob was a skeletal, white-haired man in his seventies, and I didn't want to give him a heart attack.

Bob had heard the news while watching Trish Valentine broadcasting live from the St. Paul police station. He expressed his personal sorrow and said he'd call me with an official statement in half an hour.

"I don't know if I can find a photo," he said. "Why don't you call the Royal Order of the Klondike Kates?"

"The what?" I asked.

Bob repeated the words and explained that the Kates didn't limit their performances to the Winter Carnival anymore. "They make over a hundred appearances a year at parades and benefits and even the State Fair," he said. "It's a big deal with those girls now." He gave me a phone number and said to ask for Kitty.

"Kitty Kate?" I asked.

"Kitty the coordinator," he said.

I hung up and my phone rang immediately. "She was not nude," said Martha Todd when I picked up. "You lied to me."

"Sorry. I couldn't resist," I said. "How'd you find out?"

"I just watched a rerun of Trish Valentine broadcasting live from the scene. Did you see her out there?"

"I saw her eyes and her nose. She was working undercover."

"Deep cover," said Martha.

"Gotta go," I said. "I need to call a Kate named Kitty."

A minute later I was talking to a woman who identified herself as Kitty Catalano. Again I broached the reason for my call with caution. This time I got a scream.

POLICE CHIEF CASEY O'MALLEY's 3:00 P.M. media briefing was a waste of time, but Al and I were sent as a means of showing the *Daily Dispatch* flag. Al got a picture of the chief and Detective Curtis Brown together, which was sure to score points with Brownie if it ran in the morning edition, but I learned nothing new except that the medical examiner's autopsy report wouldn't be released until Monday morning. Apparently the defrosting was taking even longer than expected.

Our only reward for attending was the appearance of Trish Valentine, reporting live. The outdoor temperature was still ten below zero, but the briefing was indoors, and we got to see Trish sans mushroom-shaped coat. Trish, who was known for her provocative wardrobe, was wearing a hot pink sweater that provided a heart-warming display of her charms. Every man present, the chief included, appreciated and admired her choice.

Back at the office, I found a woman about my age, which is a youthful forty, sitting at my desk with her long, lavender coat draped over the back of the chair. She rose, shook my hand with a surprisingly-strong grip and introduced herself as Kitty Catalano, the Klondike Kate coordinator who had screamed in my ear. After she'd recovered a modicum of aplomb, she'd promised to deliver a photo of Lee-Ann and an official statement of grief from the Royal Order of Klondike Kates.

On the phone Kitty had told me that she'd competed for the title of Klondike Kate a year ago, so I was surprised to see a woman who could pose as AFTER for one of those BEFORE AND AFTER weight-loss commercials. She was tall, close to six feet, and I surmised from the breadth of her shoulders that she was a regular at the gym.

She was wearing a white sweater and gray slacks that emphasized the sleek curves of her breasts and hips and the slenderness of her waist. A fashionable red wool cap was pushed back on her head and her slacks were tucked into western-style red leather boots that went up to the middle of her calves.

Apparently my face gave away my thoughts about her figure. "I've dropped a few pounds since last year's contest," Kitty said.

"On you it looks good," I said. "Or maybe I should say 'off you.'"

Kitty gave me a half-smile, brushed a wisp of dark-brown hair away from one of her green eyes and handed me the large manila envelope in her left hand. "Thanks," she said. "Here's the statement and the photo I promised you. If you have any questions I'll be in the office until five."

I did have questions. "How well did you know Lee-Ann?"

"I got acquainted with her after I got the job as coordinator six months ago, but I didn't know her as well as the other girls.

All the past and present Kates are pretty tight. It's like a sisterhood."

"Can you have one of the sisters who was really close to her call me?" I asked.

"I can try. It won't be a popular request."

I handed her my business card. "I'd like to be able to describe Lee-Ann as she was in life, rather than as the victim of a tragedy."

"That's nice of you. I'll tell her friends that when I ask them to call you." She shook hands, slung her coat over her arm and walked away before I could tell her how nice I really am. Every male eye in the newsroom followed her until the elevator doors closed behind her.

I opened the envelope and pulled out a color photo of a round-faced blonde with wide blue eyes, a snub nose and a dazzling smile that said she loved life. She was wearing the same short-sleeved purple dress that I'd seen in the frozen driveway.

"It's always the pretty ones that the bastards kill," said a voice behind me. I turned to face Fred Donlin, the night city editor, who'd been peeking over my shoulder.

"I can't imagine looking into this face and having the urge to kill her," I said. I handed Fred the picture and went to work on my computer, inserting the official Kates' statement into my story. I'd just punched the send button when it occurred to me that John Robertson, Jr., had never returned my call.

I punched in the Capitol number and the extension. A man answered and identified himself as Ray Walker. I asked for John Robertson and was told that he'd left for the day. "He was in early for one of those stupid sunrise breakfasts that our governor loves so much," Walker said.

"Who was the governor stuffing with doughnuts this morning?" I asked.

"Gun nuts," said Walker. "They were stuffing him with bullshit about the need for allowing folks to carry concealed weapons. Only for self-protection, of course."

A few years previously, the Minnesota gun lobby had won a well-financed campaign to allow people to carry guns in public as a means of self-protection. Facilities that wanted to be gun-free, such as churches and hospitals and gambling casinos, were required to post signs to that effect. Now the gunners were firing the next shots at their target of universal hidden armament.

"Oh, goodie," I said. "My tax dollars at work so we can all pack pistols in our armpits."

It was past time to go home. I put down the phone and picked up my coat. I had one arm in a sleeve when the phone rang. I contemplated letting it go back to the central operator but succumbed to curiosity.

"Brownhere," said the caller. "Don't you ever go home?"

"People like you keep me here at all hours," I said. "If you want, I can go home right now and you could call me there."

"I already called you there. Your sweetie said you were so late she'd been thinking about calling me to see if we had any bodies that looked like yours."

"Well, here I am, alive and relatively well. What's up?"

"I'll tell you something that you can't print yet if you'll promise to give me some help."

"What kind of help?" I asked. I rarely dealt with sources off the record. This sort of cooperation would not come cheap.

"You'll be covering a lot of the Winter Carnival crap, right?"

"Right. Of course I won't describe the gala carnival events in quite so crude a manner."

"I'm sure. What I'm asking is that you keep your eyes and ears open for anything that might be related to this morning's not-so-gala event."

"You're thinking the murder is connected to the carnival?" I asked.

"Everything points that way. Number one, the victim was last year's Klondike Kate. Number two, we've been told that the victim attended a party for the Queen of the Snows candidates last night and was later seen leaving a downtown bar with a man wearing a Vulcan costume."

"A Vulcan costume? Are you shittin' me?" I asked.

"Have I ever?"

"Not that I've ever caught you."

"Good enough. All I'm asking is that you pay close attention when the Vulcans are around. We're going to be talking to all of them individually, but we can always use another set of ears. And remember, you can't print that yet."

"Why not?" I asked. "It might get a response from somebody who saw them after they left the bar."

"It might also totally destroy the Winter Carnival," Brown said. "Can you imagine the reaction people would have when they saw the Vulcans coming if they thought one of them killed that woman?"

"Good point. I'll keep my mouth shut and watch the Vulcans like the proverbial hawk."

The latter wouldn't be difficult. Al and I had a feature story assignment to ride with Vulcanus Rex and his Krewe from morning until night the next day.

CHAPTER Four

Uneasy Rider

L ET ME EXPLAIN THE ST. PAUL WINTER CARNIVAL, which many people find inexplicable. The Carnival begins the last weekend of January and runs into the beginning of February. The scenario, in a nutshell (and you have to be a nut to come out of your shell and run around outside in Minnesota at that time of year) is this:

King Boreas, who represents the forces of snow and ice, rules the Carnival along with the Queen of Snows, who represents sugar and spice and everything nice. Vulcanus Rex and his red-clad seven-man Krewe ride around the city in an over-the-hill fire truck bringing chaos and confusion to many Carnival events. On the final night of the Carnival, the Vulcans summon warmer weather by driving away the winter king and queen, along with their retinue of princes, princesses and royal guards.

As silly as all this sounds, the Carnival attracts approximately 350,000 visitors each year and generates an estimated $3.5 to $5.0 million in economic activity, according to the press release delivered to my desk by the St. Paul Festival & Heritage Foundation.

Carnival events include toboggan runs, ice fishing contests, parades, ice sculpture exhibitions, dog team rides and, of course, the Klondike Kate Cabaret. Not bad for a celebration that began in 1886 to showcase the fast-growing city and disprove the insult written by a New York newspaper reporter who had described St. Paul as "another Siberia, unfit for human habitation in the winter."

The Vulcans have been rebuilding their image ever since a woman filed a complaint against one of the Krewe, claiming that he reached too high up her thigh while putting an honorary garter in place. Nobody would be installing any garters on the morrow. Also verboten was the traditional kiss, during which Vulcans marked the face of every available female with a greasy black smudge transferred from their cheeks and beards. The mark of the reformed, politically-correct Vulcan is a black V, made with a stick of greasepaint and applied only after asking for the fair damsel's consent.

I decided that the one exception to my no-tell promise would be Alan Jeffrey. I figured he had the right to know that he might be sharing the back end of a fire truck with a murderer. I called him at home and told him what I'd learned from Brownie.

"A Vulcan costume?" Al said. "Are you shittin' me?"

"Have I ever?" I asked.

"Lots of times."

"Well, this time I'm not. Brownie thinks one of the Vulcan Krewe might have killed Lee-Ann Nordquist. And we'll be with the Vulcans all day tomorrow."

"Why are we wasting a day with these clowns anyhow? It doesn't sound like the kind of assignment we'd get from Don."

"The stated purpose is to provide depth to our coverage of the Winter Carnival," I said. "The Vulcans are trying to polish up their image, and Don pointed out that we do have a stake in the Carnival. I suspect he was reminded of this by somebody higher up the food chain."

Our stake was a treasure hunt the paper sponsored every year. One of the guys in the advertising department hid a box containing the key to the treasure chest somewhere within the city limits and wrote a bunch of clues in verse. One of these clues would appear every day in the paper until some lucky soul found the box with the key and claimed the cash.

"Okay," Al said. "Onward and upward for Vulcan and the Carnival."

"And put on your long johns. It's going to be colder than a penguin's tail feathers tomorrow."

"Does a penguin have tail feathers or is it like the kee-kee bird?"

"What the hell is a kee-kee bird?" I asked.

"You haven't heard of the kee-kee bird? The kee-kee bird lives in the Arctic, has no feathers on its butt and sits on a cake of ice all day yelling, 'Kee, kee, kee, kee-rist but it's cold!'"

"Kee-rist, why did I ask? I'll see your sorry butt at Vulcan headquarters first thing in the morning."

The temperature had peaked at nine degrees below zero in late afternoon and was beginning its evening descent when I left the office almost twelve hours after my wakeup call from Don O'Rourke. The thermometer beside the back door of my apartment building was showing fourteen below when I arrived home. However, it was as warm as the Fourth of July inside my apartment, where I was greeted by Martha Todd and Sherlock Holmes.

Martha welcomed me with a hug and a lingering kiss. Sherlock met me with a "meow" and an invitation to scratch his furry belly.

Martha is the dark-haired, dark-eyed love of my life. She had moved in with me after completing a three-year working commitment with the attorney general in her mother's native country, Cape Verde, in payment for a law school scholarship. She has skin the color of coffee with cream, a smile so white that it puts every toothpaste ad to shame and the most exquisitely proportioned ass of any woman alive. The world's premiere sculptors could not design such an ass, and painters wouldn't even try to replicate Martha's ass because a flat image on canvas could not do justice to such three-dimensional perfection. To look upon such an ass is a privilege. To touch it was heaven on earth.

Sherlock is a fourteen-pound, short-haired, black-and-white neutered tomcat that adopted me several years ago when I made the mistake of feeding him at the back door. The three of us lived in my one-bedroom, ground-floor apartment in a two-story brick building that faces Grand Avenue.

"What a hellacious day you've had," Martha said. "Sit down and tell me all about it while we eat."

I sat across the small kitchen table from her, filled my plate with pasta, veggies, and salad, and proceeded to tell her everything. Well, almost everything. I decided that the item about one of the Vulcans with whom I'd be riding the next day possibly being a cold-blooded killer was better left unsaid. I'd had some uncomfortable moments with murderers in the past, and I saw no reason to start Martha's worry wheels whirling.

Later, sitting in bed, we watched the ten o'clock news and saw film of Lee-Ann Nordquist's rigid body being carried to the ambulance. Martha shivered at the sight and snuggled so close that she almost got inside my skin, a perfect example of how one person's great loss can be another's magnificent gain.

Despite the exhilarating contact with Martha's naked body, I was half asleep by the time she flicked off the TV. "Want to try Number 58?" she asked.

"I don't think I'm up to it," I said. "Been too long a day."

"Well, we definitely want you to be up when we go for Number 58," she said. "Nighty night, lover."

THE FORECAST FOR FRIDAY MORNING was a temperature of twenty-five below zero augmented by a blast from the northwest that again would produce a wind chill of minus forty. For once, damn it, the forecasters were right. Bundled once more in my warmest ski regalia, I forced the Civic's unwilling engine to turn over, scraped most of the windshield and persuaded the wheels to break free from the ice encrusted surface of the parking lot.

Al and I were supposed to meet the Vulcan Krewe at 9:00 in the Vulcans' Crowne Plaza Hotel headquarters. I decided to swing by the office first and found two women waiting at my desk when I arrived at 8:15. Both were wrapped in heavy, ankle-length coats, topped with bright-colored wool scarves and knit hats. At my invitation, they removed their hats, unwound their scarves and unbuttoned their coats.

The olive-skinned brunette introduced herself as Esperanza de LaTrille, and the blue-eyed, fair-skinned blonde with her nose and cheeks reddened by the cold said her name was Toni Erickson. "Kitty said you wanted to talk to some Kates who were friends with Lee-Ann Nordquist," said Toni. "We were with her the night she was . . . the night she died."

"Nice to meet you," I said as I dug a reporter's notebook out of the jumble on my desk. "Somebody else will be doing the follow story today because I've got another assignment but you can talk to me and I'll pass your comments to the desk. First of all, I need the spelling of your name, Esperanza."

"First or last?" she asked.

"Both." She gave it to me and Toni offered the information that her first name was spelled with an "I" and that she was an "s-o-n" Erickson, not "s-e-n."

"Your paper got it wrong last year when they wrote about Klondike Kate's," she said. "Called me 'Tony Ericksen,' with a 'Y' and an 'E' like I was a Danish guy instead of a nice Norwegian girl."

"We'll get it right this year," I said. "Tell me about Lee-Ann and what the three of you did Wednesday night."

"Lee-Ann is . . . was . . . one of the sweetest people you'd ever want to meet," Toni said. "She loved to be with people and to party, but she loved her little girl more than anything. I can't imagine how Sarajane is going to live without her mom."

"Word is she's with Lee-Ann's parents," I said. "Do you know if they're the kind of grandparents who appreciate their grandkids?"

"Lee-Ann left Sarajane with her folks every time she needed a baby sitter," Esperanza said. "So I'm guessing they'll give her a good loving home. But mama and daughter had a special relationship, especially after Sarajane's daddy was killed."

That got my attention. "What happened to him?"

"Afghanistan war," Toni said. "One of those goddamn roadside bombs."

"If some families didn't have bad luck they wouldn't have any luck at all," I said.

"Tell me about it," Toni said. "Lee-Ann's father lost a leg in Vietnam. Stepped on a goddamn mine."

"Next you'll tell me her mother lost an arm in some goddamn accident," I said. "She didn't, did she?"

Toni and Esperanza both shook their heads. "So tell me about Wednesday night," I said.

They said the three of them got together about 8:30 and went to a party for the Queen of the Snows candidates in the Hotel St. Paul. They had a couple of drinks, danced a couple of dances with various men and had a good time.

When that party ended, they moved on to O'Halloran's Bar, a few blocks away on Wabasha Street, along with a couple of dozen other party-goers. Among them were some men in Vulcan costumes. The three Kates, all in costume, drank, joked and played a little friendly grab-ass with several men, including the Vulcans.

"Lee-Ann and one of the Vulcans talked for a while at a separate table," Toni said. "Last I saw of her, she was going to the ladies' room. She must have gone out the back door from there."

"What about the Vulcan she was talking to?" I asked.

"Not sure," said Esperanza. "I thought he was still there because I saw three of them at the bar but Toni thought she'd seen four Vulcans so maybe one was missing."

"We just don't know if a Vulcan went out of O'Halloran's at the same time as Lee-Ann or not," Toni said.

"You didn't see them go out together?" I asked.

They both shook their heads and said, "No." I silently wondered who had seen them leave together—who had reported this to Detective Curtis Brown.

I thanked the two Kates and they left. I quickly typed the notes from our conversation into the computer, being very careful not to connect Lee-Ann with any of the Vulcans, and shipped it to Don O'Rourke for dispersal to whatever reporter would be picking up the murder story while I was riding with the possible murderer.

"See you later," I said to Don as I went past the desk on the way out.

"Look for some fresh angle on the Vulcans, will ya?" Don replied.

"No problem," I said. There'd be an extremely fresh angle whenever Brownie's suspicion could be revealed.

I met Al in the lobby of the Crowne Plaza. "Do you think one of these guys killed that woman?" he asked.

"No more than the cops do," I said.

"Don't ask them too many obvious questions, okay?" he said.

"Why? You afraid we might be next if the killer thinks we're suspicious?"

"Those guys carry guns don't they? A gun could go off accidentally on purpose."

"Only Vulcan himself has a gun, and it's not loaded. It shoots blanks."

"My Scoutmaster always said that unloaded guns were the most dangerous."

"So what do you want me to do?" I asked.

"Be prepared," Al said.

We rode the elevator to the sixth floor, knocked on the door of room 666 and waited for someone in the gaudy red costume of the Vulcans to respond.

I was startled when the door opened and we were greeted by a broad-shouldered, thirty-something man about Al's height dressed in a navy blue blazer, white shirt, black-and-red striped tie, and gray slacks. "Come in, gentlemen," he said, with a smile that revealed a row of perfectly-even teeth that must have cost his parents a bundle for orthodontia. "I'm Ted Carlson, the Vulcans' manager. I'm the one who schedules all their events. It was me you talked to when you set up your ride."

I remembered the name. We shook hands and looked around. The red costumes I'd expected to greet us were scattered around the room, worn by men drinking coffee and filling up on calorie-laden pastries. There were eight of them, seven wearing red cloaks over shiny red running suits and one, the tallest and broadest of the bunch, clad in a black suit and sporting the same scarlet cloak as the others. All wore snug red hats that fit like helmets over their ears and foreheads. Every face but one was white, the exception being a young African-American.

The black-suited man put down his coffee cup and walked—swaggered, actually—over to us. He was an inch taller and fifty pounds heavier than me, and I'm a substantial six-foot-one, 190 pounds. The pearl handle of a pistol protruded from a holster on his belt. Huge black goggles covered the upper half of his face. The bottom half was obscured by a mustache and goatee drawn in black greasepaint.

"Welcome aboard," he said in a deep growl. "I'm Vulcanus Rex, and you are now under my command. My first order is for both of you to get into costume double quick because we're hauling ass in ten minutes." He pointed toward two sets of red running suits, cloaks, and hats, and two pairs of black goggles, gloves, and boots, spread out on a bed.

I hadn't expected this. "You want us to dress like Vulcans?" I asked.

"Damn right," he said. "If you're riding with us I want you looking like us, not like a couple of ski bums. That won't kill you, will it?"

CHAPTER FIVE

Cooler than Cool

THE FIRST EVENT WE WERE SCHEDULED to attend was a children's snow sculpture contest in Como Park, an expanse of rolling, frozen hills about a ten-minute drive from downtown. Al and I, properly-garbed in red and black, were crammed into the back of the fire truck along with six red-suited Vulcans. The vehicle was the size of an overgrown pickup and the box had been cleared of whatever equipment was attached when it had been an operating ladder truck. I had read on the Vulcan Website that this four-wheeled piece of automotive antiquity was called The Royal Chariot. Great sense of humor, these Vulcans.

One red-suited member of the Krewe drove with one hand on the wheel, the other had the siren. The black-clad Vulcanus Rex rode shotgun, from where he occasionally aimed his pistol out the window toward the leaden sky and squeezed off a couple of rounds. Since no glass was shattered whenever we passed under one of the skyways that crossed most of St. Paul's downtown streets at the second-story level, I assumed he was firing blanks.

The shivering Krewe member braced against the edge of the truck box on my left introduced himself as the Duke of Klinker.

"Glad to meet you, your dukeship. What's your job?" I asked. I had read on the Website that the crew members all had fire-related names and specific tasks to perform.

"I'm the Fire King's aide de camp and herder of the flock," said the duke. "That means I make sure everyone is on board when the truck is ready to roll."

"Speaking of that, I notice that the truck rattles like a coiled diamondback looking at a barefoot hiker. How old is it?"

"It's a 1932 Luverne. Made in Luverne, Minnesota."

"Did you say 1932?"

Klinker laughed. "Don't worry. They've replaced almost every part in this old clunker but the frame. It won't conk out and leave us standing out in the cold."

"That's very comforting," I said. "It's bad enough riding out in the cold."

"You get used to it after a while. Everything gets sort of numb."

"Isn't everything getting numb the first stage of freezing to death?"

He laughed again. "Afraid you'll wind up like that Klondike Kate they found yesterday?"

"I hope not. Did you know her very well?"

Klinker straightened up and took a side step away, banging against a fellow Vulcan, and shook his head. "No," he said emphatically. "Never met her."

Before I could ask another question, the vintage Luverne groaned to a stop in front of a row of small humans, who were bundled from head to toe like Inuits on an Arctic seal hunt. Each of them stood beside a creature molded from snow. The sculptures ranged from your standard backyard snowman to realistic replicas of Spongebob Squarepants and Batman with his cape spread for take-off.

"Everybody out," yelled the Herder of the Flock, and we all jumped off the back of the truck. When my boots hit the blacktop, I was grateful to discover that I could still feel pain in my feet.

"Camera frozen solid yet?" I asked Al as he pulled his digital single lens reflex out of the bag slung over his shoulder.

"I should have one of those pocket hand warmers in my bag," he said. He aimed the camera at one of the snow sculptures and pressed the shutter release. He was rewarded with a comforting click and the appearance of an image on the viewing screen. "Pixels are still pixeling at twenty below."

"Cool," I said.

"Cooler than a frozen daiquiri at the North Pole. What are we supposed to be doing with these runny-nosed little sculptors?" There were, in fact, frosty drops of moisture on many noses and upper lips.

"I think Vulcan and the boys are going to pick the winners and smear some black V's on their faces."

"They better work fast while the grease is still smearable."

"You better shoot fast while the shutter is still clickable."

"And my clicking finger is still moveable," Al said as he started walking toward a giggling mound of Gore-Tex who had identified herself as Meghan and was being decorated with a greasepaint "V" by Vulcanus Rex.

The Krewe moved swiftly and made quick decisions while Al took pictures. I stamped my feet to maintain circulation. When all the prize winners had been greased and given medals, we were ushered into a small warming house where some of the youngsters' parents were drinking hot chocolate. Each of us was handed a cup of the steaming brown liquid, which we gulped down gratefully.

After disposing of our empty cups, Al and I collected the names of the kids he'd photographed and I asked one named Michael why he and the other kids weren't in school. It was, after all, a Friday.

"The teachers are meeting with our moms and dads," Michael said. "We got off yesterday and today both."

When we finished quizzing the kids, Al took some shots of the Krewe members applying black marks to the cheeks of all consenting women. The rate of consent was 100 percent.

"How times have changed," I said to the Duke of Klinker, recalling my mother's stories about the "good old days," when the Vulcans simply grabbed each woman and applied the mark with a kiss on the cheek. "The old way must have been a lot more fun."

"Damned women's lib," he said. "Next thing you know they'll be demanding to join our Krewe."

"They can compete for Klondike Kate," I said. "Maybe that's enough."

At the mention of Klondike Kate, the Duke of Klinker spun away from me and ordered the Krewe back into the Royal Chariot.

Klinker was the last one to climb aboard and he stayed in a back corner, the full length of the truck box away from me.

"The Duke of Klinker seems overly reluctant to discuss anything having to do with the words 'Klondike Kate,' even though he spoke them first," I said to Al.

"Could Klinker be the crumb who cold-cocked Kate?" he replied.

"Can't comment. Couldn't come up with a concrete connection."

"Can you keep quizzing Klinker?"

"Klinker quit quickly when I mentioned Kate's calamity."

"Crap," said Al.

"I concur," I said.

I turned the other way and introduced myself to the nearest red-clad warrior. He shook my hand and said he was Grand Duke Fertilious.

"Pleased to meet you," I said. "With a title like that, you must have some interesting duties."

"Well, I'm the propagator of progeny, but that's not as exciting as it sounds," he said. "It only means that I'm the Krewe member with the most kids. The sad fact is that Fertilious doesn't get to do any extra-curricular propagating."

"Too bad," I said. "I was thinking of applying for that title next year. How many kids do you have?"

"Seven. All girls."

"How many bathrooms in your house?"

Fertilious laughed. "Not enough. Sounds like you have some daughters."

"None that I know of," I said. "But my mother has three sisters and they all have daughters. I've heard plenty of complaints about competition for bathroom time."

"Maybe someday you'll have the pleasure of competing with your own daughters."

I shrugged, wondering if that would ever happen. Both Martha and I carried heavy baggage from previous marriages and were constantly struggling with the issues of trust and commitment. She'd been beaten ferociously and repeatedly by her former husband. I'd lost my first love to a speeding truck and my second love to another suitor.

Martha and I had only recently taken the step of living together. Would we be able to extend our journey to the point of having children together? That bridge was still far from being crossed.

Fertilious turned away to talk with another Vulcan and I bounced along in silence for several minutes. Then, to my surprise, I saw that we were turning onto Mississippi River Boulevard and heading in the direction of the previous day's crime scene.

I tapped Fertilious on the shoulder. "Where are we going now?" I asked.

"To the water ski show," Fertilious said.

"Water skiing? Are you serious? It's twenty below. The river's frozen solid."

"The middle of the river is open, and the idiots, I mean the exhibitionists, are water skiing out there."

"I like your original description, but I probably can't use it in the paper."

"You might get uncomplimentary phone calls."

Wondering what Fertilious's reaction would be, I said, "We're getting close to the place where they found the body of last year's Klondike Kate."

"That was awful," he said. "Did you cover that story?"

"I was the lucky reporter chosen to stand out in the cold while the cops looked at the body."

"What do you know about who killed her?" The tone was of sincere interest.

"Not much," I said. "The cops weren't saying anything concrete yesterday and I haven't been able to follow up today because of this assignment. Did you know the victim?"

"We all did," Fertilious said. "We all went to this year's contest and partied with all the Kates, past and present, afterward. Some of the guys—not including yours truly—were in a bar with Lee-Ann last night, as a matter of fact."

This might be going somewhere. "Which guys were there?"

"I heard Ashes talking about it. I'm not sure who else. You could ask around."

At that moment the truck turned off Mississippi River Boulevard and bounced down a steep, narrow road that took us to Hidden Falls Park, a flat stretch of flood plain. The driver parked near a cluster of warmly dressed people who were, indeed, watching as a boat towing a man wearing a black rubber thermal dry suit and water skis went speeding past.

"That idiot on skis must be nuts," Al said.

"Can I quote you in my story?" I asked.

"I'm making that my suggested cutline," he replied.

"Don will love that one."

"Maybe it'll slip through, like the one about the mayor saying 'diddley squat.'"

"I sure hope not," I said. Racing to finish a story minutes before deadline, a reporter (for another newspaper, thank God) wrote: "The mayor said, 'diddley squat.'" The reporter intended to insert the correct quote later. However, the story went to the copy desk in that form seconds before deadline. The copy editor skimmed quickly over the story and sent it to the composing room.

The mayor was not pleased when he read the next morning's paper. And the publisher was not pleased when he received the mayor's subsequent phone call.

The reporter and the copy editor were duly chastised and a correction was duly printed. The irony was that what the mayor actually said wasn't worth diddley squat.

We all piled out of the Luverne and the Krewe members began mingling with the crowd, which was surprisingly large given the weather. The temperature was still ten below and a numbing breeze was blowing down the river valley. Noses, mouths and cheeks were all that showed on most of the spectators. Every square inch of exposed skin was red from the cold, and clouds of steam from the watcher's exhalations swirled around their heads.

I couldn't believe what I saw on the river. A dozen people, eight men and four women, were taking turns on the skis. An announcer on a public address system was introducing the skiers and telling us where they were from and how many contests they had won. The skiers, all clad in the black dry suits, were performing on water that remained in liquid form only because it was moving too fast to freeze.

Al was standing beside me when one of the women skiers swished out of the water and onto the adjacent ice shelf, kicked off her skis and walked through the snow and ice toward a small warming hut.

"Look at her feet," Al said.

I looked. And looked again. The woman's feet were bare.

"Maybe they're frozen solid," I said. "That way she can't feel them."

Al shot a series of photos, zooming in on her feet at the end. "I've heard of keeping a woman pregnant in the summer and barefoot in the winter, but this is the first time I've ever seen the barefoot part."

Watching the skiers skim the frigid water was sadistic fun, but I was really wanting to get next to the Count of Ashes and ask him about the party where Lee-Ann Nordquist was last seen alive. However, I had two problems. The first was that I didn't know which one of the masked warriors was Ashes. The other was that all the Vulcans were busy schmoozing the female spectators and applying grease to any exposed patch of facial skin they could find. In some cases it was hard to determine who was male and who was female because of the abundance of clothing, but the Krewe moved boldly forward and more than one man got decorated with a V.

"Good thing they're not doing it the old way," Al said, nodding toward a burly man with a black smear on his cheek.

"You mean by kissing?" I asked.

"Exactly. Any Vulcan who kissed that one by mistake would probably get a fat lip in return."

"Would that be called paying lip service to your job?" I said.

"You can button your lip any time," Al said.

At that moment, the herder of the flock issued the call to board the chariot, and moving stiffly from our long exposure to the cold, we climbed aboard.

"It's back to the hotel for lunch, me hearties," Vulcanus Rex shouted as he slid into the passenger side of the cab. This sounded good to me because I could hear my feet thumping on the metal floor of the truck box but I could no longer feel them.

I clapped my hands together a dozen times to bring back feeling to my fingers as the Luverne labored up the hill to street level. When we had reached the top and were heading toward downtown St. Paul, I asked another of the red-clad Krewe which one of them was the Count of Ashes.

"At your service, sir," he said. "I am the Count of Ashes, otherwise known as the swinger of the Krewe and the raiser of Sleeping Spirits."

"The swinger of the Krewe?" I asked. "I thought all of you were swingers."

"In a sense that's true, but I'm the one you will actually see swinging upside down next Friday night at some joint on Payne Avenue. The event is called the Ashes Swing. You will be there, won't you?"

"Wouldn't miss it for all the ice in the river."

He smiled, revealing an even row of sparkling teeth. "So, prince of the printed word, why seekest thou the Count of Ashes?"

With an appreciative bow, I said, "I seekest to talkest to everyone in the Krewe while we're riding with you today. You know, give the readers a feel for the personalities involved."

"Well, as I told you, my personality involves being dumb enough to swing upside down in front of a bunch of people who are more interested in getting sloshed."

"I'm sure I couldn't do it. Are you out somewhere every night during the Carnival?"

"Pretty much," he said. "We're a busy bunch."

"Did you happen to be in the bar Wednesday night with Lee-Ann Nordquist and some of the other Klondike Kates."

The smile disappeared. "Why do you want to know?"

"I'm trying to cover two stories at once," I said. "I was there when they found Lee-Ann's body yesterday. I'll be picking up that story again after riding with you today, so I'm trying to find out as much as I can about who might have seen her that night. It's not a big deal."

"Well, I said everything I'm going to say about that night to the cops, so please don't ask me any questions about the bar scene and Lee-Ann." With that, he turned and muscled his way past two of his compatriots to the back of the truck box, where he stood next to the Duke of Klinker for the rest of the ride. Their conversation included a number of head movements in my direction, which made me feel sort of like a turkey watching the farmer sharpening his ax.

Okay, I thought, that leaves me with four other red cloaks and Vulcanus Rex himself to question during the lunch break. I didn't want to push any of them too hard, but at the very least I wanted to find out which ones had been questioned by the police. That would give me a starting point for my next chat with Detective Curtis Brown.

CHAPTER SIX

The Heat is On

MERE WORDS CANNOT CONVEY THE wonderful feeling of being inside the Crowne Plaza Hotel and immersing myself in an enduring envelope of heat. Wonderful, that is, after a brief period of needles lancing through my fingers and several minutes of knife points stabbing into my toes as my tortured digits returned from their state of cryogenic suspension.

"Thank god we're only doing this for one day," Al said as he banged his toes against the carpeted floor in an effort to restore circulation. "I can't imagine these guys freezing their asses off every day for . . . how long?"

"The carnival runs twelve days," I said. "I don't know if they're out in that damn truck every day, but I'm guessing at least ten."

"Give me a sweaty day at the Aquatennial any time," Al said.

This would be the Minneapolis Aquatennial, which occurs in August when the daytime temperatures range from eighty-five to ninety-five degrees.

"That does seem like a more appropriate time to water ski," I said.

"It's a more appropriate time to do anything outdoors. I swear my toes are frost-bitten from standing around on that cake of ice by the river."

"Think about that water skier's bare feet."

"I'm remembering how she looked in that skin-tight rubber dry suit and thinking about more than her feet being bare."

"A shocking statement by a married man," I said. Al's wife is an extremely attractive blue-eyed blonde whose figure is still svelte after giving birth to a daughter and a son.

"I'm speaking strictly as a photographer," Al said. "I constantly try to get to the bottom of things."

Vulcanus Rex and his Krewe ate lunch at a long table in the room where we'd met them that morning. As we ate, I was able to get a better look at their faces because they'd removed their hats and goggles, but I didn't recognize any of them as men who'd been featured in the news.

I was seated between Grand Duke Fertilious, blond, blue-eyed, round-faced and younger than I expected, and Baron Hot Sparkus, who was older (early forties), thinner and less willing to chat up a reporter. Fertilious wanted to question me about journalistic procedures and ethics. Hot Sparkus, who I wanted to question about Lee-Ann Nordquist's last visit to a bar, was engaged in a long conversation with Klinker, who was seated on his other side.

Our desserts were before us when I finally managed to detach myself from Fertilious and get in a word with Hot Sparkus. He was a square-faced, broad-shouldered man in his mid-thirties with bushy black eyebrows and a heavy five o'clock shadow. According to the Vulcans' Website, Hot Sparkus was "the spark plug of the Krewe," whatever that meant.

I had decided to take a less direct approach to questions about who was in the bar with the murdered Klondike Kate, so we talked about the Carnival in general, the role of Vulcans and, finally, about the role of Klondike Kate. Our conversation was pleasant and relaxed until I asked if he had been acquainted with the unfortunate Lee-Ann Nordquist.

Even this roundabout tactic failed. The man's back and shoulders went rigid. "What's Lee-Ann Nordquist got to do with your story about riding with us?" he asked.

"Nothing really, but I'm working on the murder story as well, so I'm looking for comments from people who knew her."

"You're sure she was murdered?"

"I don't think she took off her coat and laid down in that frozen driveway and died all by herself. Do you?"

"Well, it seems to me that's for the cops to determine," said Hot Sparkus. "Why don't you ask them who they think did what? Now if you'll excuse me, I'm going to take a leak."

He rose and walked off to the men's room. When he returned to the table, he sat on the opposite side, as far from me as he could get.

I had now struck out with four members of the Krewe. The only item of interest so far was the discrepancy between the responses of the Duke of Klinker, who said he'd never met Lee-Ann, and the Grand Duke Fertilious, who told me that everybody in the Krewe knew her.

Still to be approached were Count Embrious, General Flameous, the Prince of Soot and Vulcanus Rex. I rose and was heading toward one of the men I hadn't questioned when the Herder of the Flock announced that it was time to don cloaks, goggles and hats and hustle our buns out to the Royal Chariot. Foiled again.

"Where to this time?" I asked the Vulcan on my right as the truck roared out of the hotel garage with siren screaming.

"A big daycare center," he replied. "Lots of little kids. It should be fun."

"Which Krewe member are you?"

"General Flameous at your service, sir. I'm the Keeper of the Flame, which is a huge responsibility because legend has it that if the flame dies, the Fire King dies, and that would be the end of us all."

"That is a huge responsibility. I can't imagine the Winter Carnival without the Vulcans."

The general smiled and nodded in agreement. "Without Vulcanus Rex to bring him down, King Boreas would rule forever and winter would never end. St. Paul truly would become another Siberia, and it would be freezing here all year round."

"Well, take good care of that flame," I said. "Stay out of dangerous places, like parties in rowdy bars."

His smile disappeared. "If you're leading into asking me if I was in O'Halloran's the night Lee-Ann Nordquist was killed, don't bother," he said. "I've already told the cops that I wasn't there and I don't know who was."

"What makes you think I was going to ask that?"

"The word was passed at lunch that you've been nosing around about who was in the bar that night. What's the big deal about that, anyway?"

"I've been told that several Vulcans were in the bar that night. I'm working on that story and I'm wondering if any of them talked to Lee-Ann or saw anything that might be helpful in identifying the killer."

"Like I said, I don't know who was there and what's more I don't care who was there. I'm sure none of our guys had anything to do with what happened to Lee-Ann."

"I'm not implying that they did," I said. "As I said, I'm just wondering what, if anything, they saw."

"Then ask the cops who questioned them," General Flameous said. "If the cops want the press to know who was there and what they saw, the cops will tell you. You're not going to get anything from our guys so you might as well stick to the subject at hand, which right now is a visit to the daycare center we're parking at." He turned his back to me and jumped off the back of the truck the second it quit rolling.

We were in front of a sprawling, two-story, red-brick house surrounded by a four-foot-high wrought-iron fence. Arranged on the snow-covered side yard was an assortment of swings, slides, and various climbing structures in every color of the rainbow. A recently fallen layer of snow clinging to these playthings had not been disturbed, which, considering that the temperature had soared to the day's high of six degrees below zero, showed good judgment on the part of the daycare center employees.

Inside, we were greeted by about twenty screaming and giggling pre-schoolers who charged fearlessly at us, hugged us, high-fived us and generally treated us like a football team coming home after winning the Super Bowl.

I joined the Vulcans in returning the hugs and high-fives while Al shot about fifty photos. I even applied grease to a few kiddy faces and helped pass out big red-and-black metal pins with Vulcanus Rex's face on them.

"Pin one on me," shouted one of the young women overseeing the juvenile mayhem. She thrust out a substantial bosom, with the top two buttons of her blouse unbuttoned, as my target. I gingerly grasped the open edge of her blouse near a buttonhole and slid the pin into the cloth, hoping I wouldn't stab too deep. Before I could move my hands away, she pressed that substantial bosom tight against my chest, wrapped her arms around me and kissed me on both cheeks. "Hail, Vulcan!" she said when she pulled her lips away.

"Hail, Vulcan!" I said with my palms still trapped against her breast. At last I was beginning to understand why men volunteered for this job.

The woman kissed me enthusiastically again, this time on the lips, and momentarily tightened her bear hug before releasing me. "Thanks for coming," she said. "The kids just love you guys."

"And we love them," I said, resisting the urge to tell her what else I'd loved about this visit.

The Vulcans were moving toward the door, so I gave the woman a little good-bye wave and followed the river of red. Outside on the sidewalk, Al fell into step beside me. "Looks like you were keeping abreast of the action in there," he said.

"Are you going to bust me for that?" I asked.

"I do have a photo of your brave frontal advance, which would be of great interest to both your city editor and your live-in lover." He extended his camera, and in the display window I saw myself wrapped in the daycare worker's arms with my hands obviously buried against her breasts.

"But neither Don nor Martha will ever see that photo, will they?"

"Why won't they?"

"Because I'll throw your camera off the back end of the fire truck if you don't hit the delete button right now."

"You'd have to throw me with it," Al said.

"That's no problem," I said. I was three inches taller than Al, even if our poundage was roughly the same.

Al pressed the delete button. "Happy now?"

"Hit it again," I said. I knew the first press merely brought up a message asking for confirmation of the order to delete.

He frowned and pressed delete again. "It's a shame to lose the photographic record of such a historic act. I even had the perfect cutline in mind."

"And what was that?" I asked.

"Staff writer Warren Mitchell becomes a titular leader of the Vulcan Krewe."

Back in the box of the Luverne, I worked my way next to one of the two Vulcans I hadn't quizzed. There was barely enough skin showing between his goggles and his beard for me to ascertain that he was the African-American. He told me his title was Count Embrious and said he was the Fire King's Chancellor of the Exchequer. Before I could ask a single question, he said, "I'm not discussing Lee-Ann, any of the other Klondike Kates or anything I saw in O'Halloran's Bar with you."

I wondered if he realized he'd just told me that he'd been in the bar with the murdered woman. Not wishing to press my luck, I said, "I'm not going to push you on that subject. It seems like you guys have decided as a team not to answer any questions about Lee-Ann."

"You got that right," Embrious said. "You want answers, ask the cops."

"I'll do that," I said. "Thanks for your help."

I felt a nudge from the other side and turned to find myself facing the only man (with the exception of Vulcanus Rex himself)

I hadn't spoken with. "I'm the Prince of Soot," he said. "Talk to me when we get back to the hotel."

CHAPTER SEVEN

Foiled Again

THERE WAS ONE MORE STOP for the Royal Chariot before returning to the hotel. This facility's residents were at the opposite end of the age spectrum from those in the daycare center. We were parking in front of a nursing home

Although we were welcomed with smiles in the nursing home parlor, the atmosphere was not nearly as exuberant as our greeting at the daycare center. There were no high-fives, no high-pitched squeals and no little arms locking around our knees like a cowboy wrestling a roped dogie to the ground. Most of our hosts remained seated, many of them in wheelchairs, and at least half of those who stepped up to shake our hands or offer a cheek for marking did so with the aid of walkers.

The air in the daycare center had been comfortably warm and it smelled of chewing gum, chocolate, and chalk. The air in the nursing home was stifling for people dressed as warmly as we were and it smelled of . . . well, old people. I was hoping we wouldn't stay very long. Even the below-zero air outside was preferable to this.

Al was more selective with his camera work, bypassing patients whose faces remained devoid of expression in favor of those whose countenances glowed with recognition and pleasure.

"This is a place I never want to be," Al said sotto voce.

"You'd better be good to your children then," I said. "They're the ones who'll decide where you end up."

"In that case, you'd better get started on your own batch of kids or you'll be shuffled off to the cheapest place in town by some social worker you've never met."

My own batch of kids. This was the second time today that this nebulous subject had come up.

While I was trying to think of a snappy comeback, Vulcanus Rex announced that he was about to conduct "a Knighting Ceremony." From somewhere under his cloak, he produced a red, black, and gold certificate, held it aloft and called out a name. A stooped, gray-haired woman with a two-wheeled walker and a smile as wide as Alice's Cheshire cat stepped slowly forward. With great solemnity, the Vulcan leader read the certificate, which proclaimed that the woman was the mother of a previous Fire King, kissed the woman on both cheeks and handed her the certificate. "I dub you Mother of the Perpetual Flame and declare that you are a Fire King Knight forever," he said.

The woman thanked him and pressed the certificate to her bosom with one hand while gripping the walker tightly with the other. The room was filled with applause as Vulcanus turned and led us out of the stifling heat and into the stinging but welcome cold fresh air.

"That was nice," I said to Vulcanus as I passed him on my way to the rear of the Royal Chariot.

"You, too, could be knighted if the story you write about your journey with us is deemed suitably constructive," he said.

"You wouldn't be trying to bribe me, would you?" I asked.

"We hope that no bribe is necessary," the Fire King said as he climbed into the passenger seat. I wondered if he was using the royal "we" or if he was speaking on behalf of more than one member of the Krewe.

The ride from the nursing home to the hotel was blessedly short and our recovery from the cold was much quicker than it had been at noon. Al and I were finished with our assignment, but I was eager to talk with the Prince of Soot and to interview Vulcanus Rex. I was less than happy, therefore, when my pursuit of the Sooty Prince was interrupted in the lobby by Ted Carlson, the stiff in the blue blazer and red-and-black tie.

"Enjoy your day?" he asked as he popped into my path so suddenly that I almost smacked into him head-on.

"It was great if you like frozen fingers and frosty feet," I said. I tried to zig past him but he countered with a zag.

"I'll be happy to answer any questions you might have," Carlson said as I watched all eight members of the Krewe squeeze into an elevator.

"What I really want to do is get up to the Vulcans' suite and change back into my own clothes," I said.

"Me, too," Al said as the elevator door was closing.

"Oh, your clothing has been brought down to a room just off the lobby," Carlson said. "You can change in there while I answer your questions."

"I'd also like to talk to Vulcan and some of the other Krewe members a little bit," I said.

"They're about to have a private meeting," Carlson said. "I'm sure I can answer any questions you might have. Follow me, please." He turned and led us toward a hallway to the left of the registration desk.

"I think we've been sandbagged," Al said. "You've asked the wrong question of too many people."

"I think you're right," I said. "My only hope is to find out where they're going next and try to catch the Prince of Soot there."

Carlson stopped in front of a first-floor room, unlocked the door and ushered us in, practically bowing and scraping as we entered.

"What are they meeting about?" I asked.

"They always like to compare notes at the end of the day and prepare for the evening schedule," Carlson said. "Your clothes are on the bed, and I'm here ready to answer any and all questions."

I was tempted to ask which Krewe members had been in O'Halloran's Bar Wednesday night but I knew he'd pass on that one. "Where are they going after dinner?" I asked instead.

"After dinner they'll be going to Klondike Kate's," he said.

"Klondike Kate's is still going to be open after the, uh, after what happened the other night?" Al asked.

Carlson smiled a promoter's smile. "This is the Winter Carnival," he said. "You know the old saying, the show must go on."

"The show at Klondike Kate's would seem to be a lot less fun," I said.

"There will be some changes in the program," Carlson said, looking appropriately sober. "They're opening with a solemn moment in memory of Ms. Nordquist. And I suspect the atmosphere will be a bit quieter than usual."

"Until everybody gets drunk," Al said.

"I assure you that Vulcan and his Krewe will remain sober," Carlson said. "Our current Fire King has expressly forbidden excessive drinking by the Krewe."

"Speaking of that, can you give me a list of the Krewe's real names?" I asked.

"I'm afraid not," he said. "The identity of Vulcan and his Krewe is never revealed until King Boreas is banished at the climax of the carnival."

"We have to wait for Vulcan to climax?" Al said."

Carlson's ears turned an interesting shade of pink. "Correct," he said after a slight pause. "I'm sorry, but this is the Winter Carnival and tradition is tradition."

"And the show must go on," I said.

The smile returned to Carlson's face. "Absolutely right," he said. "Now, do you have any other questions?"

"Not at the moment," I said. "Can I reach you tomorrow morning in case I need something while I'm writing the story?"

"I'll be here in the hotel. Here's my card with my cell phone number. I always have it turned on."

I took the card and thanked him. He said if we had no further questions he would leave us in private to get dressed. We both shook his hand and bade him farewell.

"Does he think we're embarrassed to strip to our skivvies in front of him?" Al asked after Carlson left.

"Maybe he thinks we need to be alone to compare notes and prepare for our evening schedule."

"That was total bullshit," said Al.

"My thoughts exactly," I said.

OUR EVENING BEGAN WITH MARTHA and me dining with the Jeffrey family at their Midway area abode. Dinner followed by conversation or games or a DVD movie was becoming a Friday routine, but on this night Al and I were going to Klondike Kate's. We invited the women to join us in this adventure, but they chose playing games with the children, Kristin and Kevin, over frolicking with us at Klondike Kate's. Under the circumstances, I thought it was a damn smart choice—the one I'd have made if I'd had the option.

Whatever. We dutifully kissed Carol and Martha goodbye and went off to pretend to have fun, me with a tiny tape recorder in my shirt pocket and Al with his smallest digital camera in his.

CHAPTER EIGHT

Whooping it Up

THE BOOMING VOICE OF THE NEWLY-ANOINTED Klondike Kate, Angela Rinaldi, was calling upon the crowd to observe a moment of silence for Lee-Ann Nordquist when Al and I walked into the cabaret. The room fell quiet, and after an appropriate interval Angela broke the spell by observing that, as a faithful and fun-loving Kate, Lee-Ann would want the celebration to go on. Therefore, the bar was declared open and the ensemble that accompanied the singers was ordered to commence playing the "Beer Barrel Polka."

Angela was joined immediately by the two Kates who had visited me that morning, Toni Erickson and Esperanza de LaTrille, and they began to sing with as little gusto as you'd expect from three women who'd just lost a good friend. But they were troupers, and after a couple of listless verses they began to loosen up, whereupon the atmosphere in the cabaret improved from funereal to banal.

We seated ourselves at a table, and when an angular, blue-eyed blonde who introduced herself as Britney appeared and said she would be our server, we ordered a tap beer for Al and a ginger ale for Mitch the recovering alcoholic. After Britney delivered the drinks, we sipped them slowly, listening to the music and wondering when the Vulcans were going to come storming in.

Our glasses were almost empty, and Britney was looking our way, hoping to be summoned for a refill, when Al said, "Our frost-bitten buddies must have a lot to talk about over in the Crowne Plaza."

"Maybe Brownie called them downtown to ask some more questions," I said.

"Oops! Speak of the devil, or in this case, devils," Al said as the door swung open and eight scarlet-cloaked, black-booted men stomped in, waving their arms and shouting, "Hail, Vulcan!" They spread through the crowd like legs on a spider, repeating the salutation and applying a greasy V to the cheek of every woman they encountered. Nobody rejected the markings and some turned the other cheek for a duplicate decoration.

The energy level in the room soared, the trio of Kates onstage sang louder and lustier, and I was reminded of the Robert Service poem that began with, "A bunch of the boys were whooping it up in the Malamute saloon." The only thing missing was Dangerous Dan McGrew, and for all I knew one of the whooping Vulcans could be his evil equal.

"Well, the Fire King sure warmed things up," Al said as Britney approached our table with an expectant smile.

"I'd like to put a little heat on him," I said.

"Another round, gentlemen?" Britney asked.

"Why not?" Al replied. "We might as well join the party."

"Nothing worse than a party pooper," I said. "Bring me another one of those exotic ginger ales."

Britney hustled away and Al slipped the palm-sized camera out of his pocket. "Might as well take a few shots of the festivities," he said. "If nothing else, it'll justify these beers on my expense account." He moved away to a corner where he could get a better view of the crowd.

I was thinking about the Prince of Soot's offer to talk with me and I looked around the room hoping to spot him. My search was unsuccessful because even in the dim light of Klondike Kate's Cabaret the Vulcans were wearing their dark goggles, so they all looked alike. I remembered the Prince of Soot being shorter than I was, but the same could be said for four other members of the Krewe.

"Can you pick out the Prince of Soot?" I asked when Al returned.

"Are you kidding?" Al replied. "I can't tell Soot from Ashes anymore than you can tell your ash from a hole in the ground."

Britney was setting the drinks on the table, and she gave him a look that would have shriveled a grape into a raisin before she walked away.

"Soot is older than the rest of them, but with those damn goggles on they all look like Satan," I said.

"The devil, you say."

"Yes, and I also say that this is turning into one hell of a job."

"Well, it's about to take a turn either up or down," Al said, looking past me. "One of our jolly Satans is headed this way."

I turned to see one of the shorter Krewe members weaving through the crowd in our direction. He grabbed an empty chair from another table, slid it into place beside me and sat down. "Hail, Vulcan," I said.

"Very good," said the man in red. "In case you don't recognize me, I'm the Prince of Soot. If you remember, I spoke to you this afternoon."

"I do remember," I said. "In fact, I've been trying to pick you out of the crowd."

"That's the wonderful thing about these costumes," he said. "You can pull off all kinds of crap and nobody knows which one of us to blame."

I wanted to ask if "all kinds of crap" included murder, but I knew that question would bring the conversation to an abrupt halt. Instead, I said, "What do you want to talk about?"

"The same thing you were trying to talk about all during the ride," Soot said. "I want to warn you not to jump to any conclusions about who did what in O'Halloran's."

"What do you mean?"

"Look around the room for a minute."

I looked. Then I looked back at the Prince of Soot. "Okay, what am I supposed to be seeing?"

"How many red suits do you see?" he asked.

"There should be seven, including yours, plus Vulcanus Rex in a black one."

"I didn't ask how many there should be. I asked how many do you see?"

I looked again. To my amazement, I saw more than seven. "There's a dozen. What's going on?"

"Former Vulcans," the Prince of Soot said. "We get to keep our costumes at the end of the carnival. Sometimes some of the old Krewe members put theirs on and join the fun."

"So, what you're saying is that all the Vulcans seen in O'Halloran's last Wednesday night might not have been members of the current Krewe?" I asked.

"Yes, that's what I'm saying."

"That broadens the list of suspects seen at O'Halloran's to . . . how many?"

The prince shrugged. "More than you can count on your fingers and toes."

"And you're sure whoever was hanging around with Lee-Ann Wednesday night wasn't a member of your Krewe?"

"I didn't say that." He rose and saluted me. "Have a good evening, Prince of the Printed Media." With that, he walked away to join Vulcanus Rex, the only one I could positively identify because of his black running suit.

Al, who had been circulating and quietly taking photos while Soot and I talked, returned to the table. "What did old Sootie have to say?"

I told him.

"Oh, shit," Al said.

"My thoughts exactly."

We finished our drinks and were about to ask Britney for our check when another Vulcan emerged from the mob and plopped himself down in the chair vacated by the Prince of Soot. "Hi," he said. "Recognize me?" The voice sounded familiar but I'm not good at reconstructing faces around mouths and noses, which were all that showed between the man's goggles and grease-paint beard.

"Sorry," I said. "Can I have three guesses?"

"Are you sure we've met?" asked Al.

The masked man's mouth formed a smile and the teeth gave him away. "My first guess is Ted Carlson," I said.

"Very good, Mitch," Carlson said. "You could be a detective. Are you boys having fun?"

"We *men* are having a blast," Al said. "The crowd in here is pretty lively considering recent events."

"The show must go on," Carlson said. "Anything more I can do for you boys?"

My immediate response was to say he could kiss my boyish ass, but I restrained myself, knowing I might have to ask this condescending little prick a question or two in the morning while I was writing my story. "Nothing for now," I said.

"I must confess that I'm surprised to see you boys here," Carlson said. "I thought you'd be working on your story and printing your photos tonight."

"I've got plenty of time to write in the morning," I said.

"And we don't print photos anymore," Al said. "You've maybe heard of digital photography?"

"Oh, of course," he said. "Silly me."

"I must confess that I'm surprised to see you in a Vulcan costume," I said.

"You shouldn't be," Carlson said. "I was a member of the Krewe three years ago. I still love to put on the suit when there's a party."

"Been to many parties this week?" Al asked.

"Actually, I dressed up for the Queen of Snows dance Wednesday night," Carlson said. "Had a ball, if you'll pardon the pun." Again he flashed the perfect row of teeth.

"Did you go along with the crowd afterward?" I asked.

Carlson realized that the question was loaded. "If you mean the crowd that went to O'Halloran's, the answer is no," he said after a moment's pause. "I decided it was time to pack it in, so I went home."

"How late was it?" I asked.

"Late enough," Carlson said, pushing back the chair and rising. "It's been nice talking to you boys. If you have any questions in the morning, don't hesitate to call. Have a good night."

"You, too," Al and I said in unison as he walked away.

"What an asshole," Al said when Carlson was out of earshot. "Do you think he could be the extra Vulcan that one of your Kates saw in O'Halloran's?"

"Anything is possible," I said. "But I have no idea what his motive for killing Lee-Ann might be."

"He could have picked her up at O'Halloran's, took her somewhere and tried to screw her, and got rough when she wouldn't put out."

"That's possible. But we won't know whether she was sexually assaulted until we hear the ME's report on Monday. Meanwhile, I'll put him on my list of suspects."

Britney was standing beside us. "Another round, gentlemen?"

"No thanks, just the check," Al said.

"But thanks for calling us gentlemen," I said. "Our last visitor thought we were underage." I added an extra dollar to my share of the tip.

CHAPTER NINE

Autopsy-turvy

WHEN I WALKED INTO THE LOBBY of the *Daily Dispatch* building a few minutes before 8:00 a.m. on Monday, I heard loud male voices and saw a man waving a snub-nosed pistol in front of Harry, our security guard. The security desk was the first thing a visitor encountered when entering our building, and unless one wore an ID tag, one must be identified and tell Harry what department one wants to visit.

The man waving the pistol was shouting something about not giving a shit about the sign saying no firearms allowed in this building. "This gun is the whole purpose of my fucking visit," he yelled.

My first thought was to go back outside and call 911, but I quickly recognized the gun waver from the rear, which was as wide as my grandmother's antique wash tub. His name was Sean Fitzpatrick, and he was the head of an organization called the League of Effective Gun Owners, otherwise known as LEGO. I thought this acronym was extremely appropriate because the members of LEGO thought of their guns as playthings.

Fitzpatrick was in his middle fifties, with a gleaming bald head, a bulbous red nose and a belly that hung far over his belt as a result of absorbing countless kegs of beer. He was a frequent writer of letters to the editor opposing any and all gun laws, and an occasional indignant visitor to the newsroom when a story about gun control pissed him off. This was the first time I'd seen him carry a weapon into the building.

I hustled up alongside him. "Hey, Sean, what's going on?" I said. "How come you're giving Frank a hard time?"

"I'm trying to explain to this donkey that I'm here to talk about this gun," Sean said. "I want to show it to the asshole who wrote that anti-gun editorial in Sunday's paper and the other asshole that drew the stupid cartoon that went with it."

"Frank's just doing his job, Sean," I said. "According to the law that you helped push through, we have a right to ban guns in this building."

"But this is a fucking exception," Fitzpatrick yelled. "I can't explain what I want to explain if I don't show those assholes the kind of gun I'm talking about."

"Hey, Tex, cool down," said another voice. It was Al, who had just come in the door. He always tried to ruffle Fitzpatrick's feathers by calling him Tex or Gunslinger.

"Oh, great, now I'm triple-teamed by the leftwing, patriot-hating media," Fitzpatrick said. "I might as well go home."

"Oh, bullshit! What's your problem?" Al asked.

"Your dumbass editorial writer wrote a piece attacking the concealed weapons bill and your equally dumbass cartoonist drew a picture of a woman pulling an AK-47 out from between her boobs," Fitzpatrick said. "I want to show them the size of gun we're really talking about in this bill." He waved the pistol toward us and I saw it was only about five inches long.

"Is that a gun or a cigarette lighter?" I asked.

"That's what I'm trying to get across to you dumbfucks in the media," Fitzpatrick said. "People don't conceal guns any bigger than this one. It's a Derringer. A two-shot Cobra Derringer."

"You're sure it's not loaded?" Al asked.

"Of course it's not loaded," Fitzpatrick said. "I know better than to bring a loaded gun in here."

"Show me," Al said.

Fitzpatrick pushed out the cylinder so we could see that it was empty.

"How about if I take the gun and go with you to the editorial page editor?" Al asked. "I think Frank might allow that, being as how I work here and he sees me every day." Frank, who was delighted to be taken off the hook, nodded in vigorous affirmative.

The three of us rode up the elevator to the fourth floor. When we got there, I headed for my desk, and Al walked Sean Fitzpatrick through the newsroom to the editorial page office after getting everyone's attention by yelling, "Armed and dangerous gunslinger on the floor."

On my desk was a note to call Ted Carlson and a scrap of paper informing me that the ME would release the autopsy report on Lee-Ann Nordquist at 9:00 a.m. On my voice mail was a message from Kitty Catalano saying she thought my Sunday story on our ride with the Vulcans was "really super."

Ted Carlson could jolly well wait in line. I'd phone Kitty later to hear first-hand, possibly at lunch, how really super she thought my story was, but my first call had to be to Detective Curtis Brown.

He picked up after only three rings. "Homicidebrown."

"Dailydispatchmitchell. What's new on the late Klondike Kate?"

"The autopsy report," Brownie said. "Didn't you get the word?"

"I did. But there must be more than that. Surely your detectives have not been sloughing off over the weekend."

"You can tell the taxpayers that we've been working very hard on this case. However, we haven't turned up much beyond a shitload of Vulcans as possible persons of interest, which is still off the record by the way. I'm hoping you can help reduce the number from your contacts with the Vulcan menagerie. Good story and pix, by the way."

"Thanks from both me and Al," I said. "I'm sure you already know the names of three members of this year's Krewe who were in O'Halloran's."

"I do," Brownie said. "It's the possible fourth one we haven't come up with. Either the woman who thought she saw four Vulcans was seeing double from too many drinks or there was a ringer in the group."

"If there was a ringer, it could have been a guy named Ted Carlson."

"The Vulcans' manager?"

"That's the one. Have you questioned him?"

"No. What makes you think I should?"

"He talked to us at Klondike Kate's Friday night, dressed up in his Vulcan suit from three years ago. He let slip that he was at the Queen of the Snows dance Wednesday night, also in costume. He said he didn't go with the bunch to O'Halloran's, but people have been known to lie."

"Not to a reporter," Brownie said, feigning utter shock.

"Even to a reporter," I said.

"Thanks for the lead, Mitch. I'll have a little chat with Mr. Carlson. Have a good day." Brownie was gone before I could ask another question. I put down the phone realizing that I'd received nothing useful in exchange for my tidbit of intelligence. I could only hope that the ME's report was more than routine.

THE ME's REPORT WAS PRESENTED to a milling cluster of Twin Cities newspaper, television and radio reporters, along with their associated photographers and cameramen, by Police Chief Casey O'Malley. The report began with the customary facts about the cause of death, which in this case was strangulation. No surprise there.

This mundane beginning was followed by the equally stunning revelation that marks on the victim's neck indicated the use of some sort of rope as a garrote. This drew an appropriate silent response.

Next came the word that the victim's coat, hat, and scarf had been found in O'Halloran's cloakroom, which meant she'd been taken outside in below-zero weather without them. I raised my hand at this, and was told to hold my question until the chief was finished.

The time of death was estimated at between 11:00 p.m. and midnight. This was the time a witness had reported seeing her leaving through the backdoor, which led to an adjacent parking ramp, with a male companion. The fact that the companion was dressed in a Vulcan costume was not mentioned by the chief.

"Tests showed that the alcohol level in the victim's blood was .10," the chief continued. "This, of course, is above the level of legal intoxication, which is .08."

Next we were told that the victim showed signs of "vaginal bruising" but that no semen was found. If rape had been attempted, the act was not completed. Finally, the chief called for questions.

Again my hand shot up. "Does the fact that she wasn't wearing her coat indicate that she was killed immediately after leaving the building?" I asked.

"That's a possibility," said Chief O'Malley.

I followed up. "How about inside the building? Could she have been dead when the witness saw her leave with the man?" That brought a burst of verbal response from the crowd and I heard Trish Valentine say, "Gross!"

"That's also a possibility," the chief said. More groans from the masses.

"Can you identify the witness who saw her leave?" the Channel 5 reporter asked.

"The witness will not be identified at this time," Chief O'Malley said.

"Do you think the fact that the victim was legally drunk had anything to do with her death?" Trish Valentine asked.

"It may've been a factor," the chief said. "The witness who saw her leave stated that she was leaning heavily on her companion."

"What happened to her car?" asked the man holding a Channel 7 microphone. "Was she driving that night?"

"She was not driving," Chief O'Malley replied. "She lived in an apartment downtown and walked to both the dance and the party in O'Halloran's. Her car was found in her designated space in the building's parking ramp."

The chief answered a couple more questions, and when no more queries were forthcoming he said, "Oh, there is one more thing. The victim was approximately three months pregnant."

Well, didn't that start the questions and answers flying? No, the police didn't know who the father was. Yes, the fetus's DNA would be analyzed. No, neither the victim's parents nor any of her friends who police had questioned knew who she'd been seeing. Yes, the police were calling for the father to come forward voluntarily.

When the hubbub had ended and Al and I were back on the sidewalk, where the temperature was a balmy five below, I saw a woman ahead of us wearing a long lavender coat and a fashionable red cap. "Kitty!" I yelled.

Kitty Catalano stopped and turned around. "Oh, hi," she said. She forced a smile and offered each of us a black-gloved hand for shaking.

"Thanks for the phone call," I said. "I planned to get back to you later. Were you at the autopsy report?"

"Yes, I was," she said. "We're all terribly interested in finding out anything we can about poor Lee-Ann. Isn't it awful that she was pregnant?"

"It is," I said. "Two lives wasted instead of one. I don't suppose you have any idea who she might have been seeing?"

"None. Like I told you, I really didn't know her all that well. Apparently Toni and Esperanza weren't able to help the police, either, and I think they were her two best friends in the world."

"Can you think of anybody else she was close to?"

"Oh, God, I don't know. Maybe Hillary Howard. She's another Klondike Kate."

"Could you have her call me?" I asked.

"Sure," Kitty said. "A bunch of us are having lunch to discuss what we can do for Lee-Ann's family. I'll talk to Hillary then, if that's okay."

"That's fine," I said. There went the prospect of brightening my day by lunching with a beautiful woman.

Oh, well, I thought, things could be worse. And I'd no sooner sat down at my desk than they got worse. The phone rang, I answered and the doleful voice said, "This is Morrie."

Every newspaper has a timewaster like Morrie, who called to talk nonsense when a reporter was digging into something important. Our Morrie was a dumpy, disheveled, middle-aged man who walked around downtown with a little shaggy white dog on a leash. Usually he phoned to complain about the Russians watching him on radar. Sometimes the calls were about someone named Robinson, who Morrie claimed was trying to kill him. For some reason, the little kook usually asked for me.

This call had to do with Robinson. "If you put something in the paper, Robinson would be scared and leave me alone," Morrie said.

"Get a pencil and paper, I know just the person you need to talk to," I said, flipping through the scribbled scraps of paper on my desk. "Call this number." I gave him the number and extension of the Minneapolis Enquirer Capitol Bureau. Let John Robertson, Jr., deal with the Robinson dilemma.

It was mid-afternoon when Hillary Howard called. Dave Jerome, our editorial cartoonist, was sitting on that tiny uncluttered area at one corner of my desk telling me about his morning conversation with Sean Fitzpatrick when I got the call.

"It's a good thing that Al was the one carrying the gun," Dave said. "If that redneck bastard had come in with a gun in his hand I'd have been under the drawing table having a heart attack."

"I got the impression that Sean didn't care much for your cartoon," I said.

"Some people don't understand that cartoonists exaggerate things for effect. And gun nuts in particular don't have any sense of humor."

"Sean certainly didn't get a bang out of your AK-47."

"I'm just glad his little show-and-tell gun wasn't loaded or he might have shot off more than his mouth." When my phone rang, Dave waved goodbye and slid off the desk.

Like all of the women chosen to be Klondike Kate, Hillary had a strong voice. It was so strong, in fact, that I was obliged to hold the receiver an inch away from my ear when she spoke. We exchanged greetings, and I expressed my sympathy for the loss of her friend before I asked Hillary if she had any knowledge of Lee-Ann's love life.

"I knew Lee was seeing some guy she really liked," Hillary said. "But she never mentioned his name."

"Did she tell you anything about him?" I asked.

"Not much. He must have been pretty good in bed because she was always full of piss and vinegar after she'd been with him. She never actually said it, but I got the impression that the reason their relationship was such a big secret was because the guy was married."

"Did you know she was pregnant?"

"No. I don't think anybody did."

"Not even the boyfriend?"

"Who knows? Maybe she told him and he decided to kill her."

"That's possible," I said. "It wouldn't be the first time a married man knocked off a knocked-up mistress."

"That's a pretty crude way of putting it," Hillary said.

"I'm noted for being crude. It goes with the job. Do you know anything else at all about this guy?"

"No, I don't think so. Sorry."

"That's okay. You've given me a little something I didn't have before."

We exchanged goodbyes, and I put down the phone.

"Man, who was that?" asked Bob Anderson, the reporter at the desk beside mine. "Was she talking through a megaphone?"

"She doesn't need one," I said. "She's one of the Klondike Kates." Bob, who had pursued the story of Lee-Ann's murder while I was riding with the Vulcans on Friday, nodded in understanding.

I added what Hillary had told me to my Lee-Ann Nordquist computer file and was thinking about calling it a day when the phone rang again.

"It's Hillary," said the booming voice. "I just thought of something else."

"I'm all ears," I said, holding the phone an inch away from the left one.

"I'm pretty sure the secret boyfriend was a Vulcan."

CHAPTER TEN

Monday Musings

ON MONDAY NIGHTS I USUALLY went to an Alcoholics Anonymous meeting a few blocks from my apartment building. After each meeting, I had a ginger ale in a Grand Avenue establishment called Herbie's Bar & Grill with a fellow alcoholic named Jayne Halvorson. We both found it therapeutic to sit drinking in a bar without ordering alcohol.

Martha had no problem with these après meeting tête-à-têtes because Jayne had neither the time for nor the interest in becoming a romantic rival. She's about ten years older than I am, and was supporting and raising two teenage daughters all alone because her uncontrollable drinking prompted her husband to disappear before she gave herself to AA. She was always a great listener and sometimes a sage adviser.

On this particular Monday, I needed to vent about the Lee-Ann Nordquist murder.

"So, what do you know so far?" Jayne asked.

"I know that two other Klondike Kates were with Lee-Ann at O'Halloran's, and one of them says she saw three Vulcans there and the other one is sure she saw four. I know the Krewe names of three men who were in O'Halloran's that night, but the carnival brass won't release their real names until after the carnival ends.

"A witness that the cops won't identify saw Lee-Ann go out the back door with a Vulcan. She was leaning heavily on him, which could either have been because she was drunk, which she definitely was, or dead, which I think she probably was. Her hat and coat were left inside O'Halloran's, which tells me that she most likely was killed inside the building.

"She was three months pregnant, but nobody, including her two best friends, knew she was pregnant or knows who the father might be. Another one of her friends told me that Lee-Ann was seeing a man who is possibly married and is probably a Vulcan. This guy could be the prime suspect if the cops can find out who he is. But even Brownie isn't telling me anything I can print, so where do I go from here when my city editor hollers for a story tomorrow morning?"

"Seems to me you need to talk to those three Vulcans that you know were in O'Halloran's," Jayne said.

"Wish me luck with that. The whole Krewe moved away from me like an Amish family shunning a backslider when I started asking what they'd seen that night. If I knew the real names of those three turkeys, I could camp on their doorsteps, but I'm S-O-L on that until after Saturday night's big battle with Boreas. Plus, I promised Brownie I wouldn't wreck the carnival by writing about the Vulcan factor before the fun is over."

"You really are up a creek without a paddle."

"Paddle, hell. I'm up a creek without even a canoe," I said.

"Why don't you talk to the dead woman's two best buddies again?" Jayne said "Maybe they know more about the boyfriend than they're telling the police."

"You think they're protecting the guy, even though he could be the killer?"

"Stranger things have happened. People sometimes do irrational things in times of crisis."

"Wouldn't it be even more irrational for them to tell me something they didn't tell the cops?"

"They might perceive you as less threatening than Detective Brown."

"Well, they could be fun to talk to. Especially the dark and dynamic Esperanza."

"You'd better not have too much fun with Esperanza or Martha will come down on me for suggesting that you talk to those women."

"It's always strictly business," I said. "You know me."

"I do know you," Jayne said. "That's why I'm flying the caution flag."

MARTHA MET ME AT THE APARTMENT door with a rib-crunching hug and a long, long, long kiss. "Did any of your friends at AA give you any suggestions about solving the Klondike Kate mystery?" she asked when we finally came up for air.

"Jayne suggested I talk to Lee-Ann's two best buddies again to see if they'll tell me anything about the father of the baby that they wouldn't tell the cops," I said. "Other than that, I'm up against a stone wall and Don is going to be hollering for a fresh lead before I get to my desk tomorrow morning."

"Hard to believe that none of her close friends know who she was sleeping with."

"That's what Jayne said. But if those two do know anything, I can't imagine why they wouldn't tell Brownie."

"You never know what goes on in people's minds. Want to watch the ten o'clock news and see what your favorite roving blonde is reporting live?"

"Why not?" We sat snuggled together on the sofa and were joined by Sherlock Holmes, who tried unsuccessfully to squeeze between us, as we watched the news on Channel 4. Sherlock wound up stretched across both our thighs, which was truly the feline lap of luxury. As expected, we saw a clip of Trish Valentine reporting from the autopsy press conference. We even heard my voice asking about the possibility of Lee-Ann being killed inside O'Halloran's and carried out dead, but the editor had excised Trish's "gross" between my question and the police chief's answer.

"Ready to try position Number 60?" Martha asked when I turned off the TV. We had successfully negotiated Numbers 58 and 59 of the 101 positions over the weekend, and I was feeling proud of my recuperative powers.

"Of course, I'm ready," I said. "There's nothing like having new worlds to conquer."

"Think you can make my world move?"

"My down to earth answer is yes."

"Good," said Martha. "You get the book while I get naked."

Tʀᴜᴇ ᴛᴏ ғᴏʀᴍ, Cɪᴛʏ Eᴅɪᴛᴏʀ Dᴏɴ O'Rᴏᴜʀᴋᴇ stopped me before I reached my desk Tuesday morning and ordered me to produce something fresh on the killing of Klondike Kate. I told him what I had in mind, and he said if I came up with the name of the possible father he'd send Al out to get the guy's picture.

"What if the guy gets nasty?" I asked.

"That's why I'm sending your twin," Don said. "He's the fastest runner on the photo staff."

When Kitty Catalano answered at the Klondike Kate Hotline, I asked if I could talk to Esperanza and/or Toni. Kitty said Toni was with Lee-Ann's family and Esperanza had been obliged to spend some time at her day job in the loan office of a downtown bank. I called the number that Kitty gave me, and Esperanza said she could meet me for a few minutes at a coffee shop in the skyway during her mid-morning break. This meant I had two hours to search other avenues.

The first avenue I chose was Brownie. "Homicidebrown-holdtheline," he said. I held for more than five minutes with the phone cradled on my shoulder, twisting two paperclips into an approximation of Swami Sumi's Position No. 60, which had kept me awake well past midnight.

"What can you tell me about Klondike Kate this morning?" I asked when Brownie returned.

"She's still dead," Brownie said.

"That'll make a banner headline."

"On the record, we're working very hard on this case, following a number of leads. Off the record, those leads are taking us nowhere. We've quietly interrogated all the Vulcans twice, which you can't put in the paper, and three of them admit to being in O'Halloran's but say they did nothing involving the victim and saw nothing happening to the victim. The others deny having been there at all. We brought in that Carlson character you suggested and got a very indignant denial when we asked if he had gone to O'Halloran's. Says his wife will substantiate the fact that he was home long before Ms. Nordquist was seen leaving the bar. The upshot is that we still don't know if there really was a fourth Vulcan in the joint or if one of the three who admit to being at the scene could be our man. I'd like to use a rubber hose on the whole batch of them."

"Bring back the good old days," I said. "Any leads on the father of the baby?"

"Nothing yet. The lab is working on DNA samples we got from all the Vulcans by giving them glasses of water during our chats with them. We've had a few crank calls about the baby, including a couple of creepy women telling us that Lee-Ann got what she deserved because she had sinned against God by having sex out of wedlock. Nice folks, these fundamentalists."

"Probably jealous of any woman married or otherwise who has a happy sex life."

"Exactly. That leaves me with nothing new to tell you except that the ME has released the body so the family can plan a funeral."

"Do you know when and where it will be?"

"Not yet. She's at O'Dell & Son if you want to call and ask. Have a good day."

I called O'Dell & Son and was told that services would be held at 11:00 a.m. on Thursday, with a calling hour starting at 10:00 a.m. I wrote it on my calendar and went to tell Al. I thought we both should be there, checking out the crowd.

"It's a date," Al said. "There's nothing like a good, rousing visitation and funeral service to brighten up a workday morning."

"Just be glad it's not your own," I said.

"Speaking of that, Don says you're setting me up to get clobbered by the late Klondike Kate's lover boy."

"It wasn't my idea. He says you're the only one in the department who can outrun the guy after shooting his picture."

"Oh, now I'm supposed to run races with my subjects? Let's just hope this one's not a photo finish," Al said.

"That could have negative results for you," I said.

I'D FINISHED READING THE FUNNIES and was about to head for the skyway to meet Esperanza when my phone rang. "Newsroom, Mitchell," I said.

"This is John Robertson, Jr.," said an angry male voice. "Are you the Mitchell who gave my number to a nut cake named Morrie?"

"I'm the one," I said. "Did you enjoy the conversation?"

"He called me twice yesterday and again this morning, bitching about the Russians and their radar. Why the hell don't you keep your nut cakes to yourself?"

"It's to help with your OJT. I was told you're trying to learn about all the jobs at the paper before you become your daddy's right-hand man as associate publisher. Part of a reporter's job is to deal with nut cakes."

"That part I don't need. You send me any more of your wack jobs and I'll come over there and bust your face."

"If you trip over any dead bodies on the way, take a minute to call your city desk," I said. I put the phone down gently without waiting to hear his response and went to meet Esperanza.

As usual on a cold winter day, the downtown sidewalks were almost devoid of traffic, but two stories above them the skyway was swarming with pedestrians. St. Paul claims that its complex of glassed-in bridges, which lace together forty-seven city blocks, forms the biggest skyway system in the world. Residents of the condos on Wacouta Street at the eastern end can walk indoors all the way to St. Peter Street eight blocks away on the west, and to Seventh Street on the north and Kellogg Boulevard on the south. The system has grown so complex that directional signs have been posted to keep people from getting lost in the maze.

Esperanza and I arrived simultaneously at the coffee shop. She looked smashing in a burgundy jacket, white blouse, and black skirt. Or maybe the skirt was navy blue. I was never sure unless the colors were side by side. Her hair, which I was positive was black and not blue, flowed in waves down to her shoulders, setting off the olive tone of her complexion. We each ordered a medium black coffee and a chocolate doughnut.

"My worst weakness," she said, holding up the doughnut. "Without these I'd be ten pounds lighter."

I smiled and took a sip of coffee. "Chocolate is one of the government's basic food groups, isn't it?"

"It is for me," she said. "But you didn't ask to meet me just to talk about calories. What can I do for you?"

I immediately thought of something that Martha wouldn't approve of, but I didn't have time for flirting. "I'm wondering if you have any idea at all who the father of Lee-Ann's baby might be."

She took a swallow of coffee before she answered. "I've already told the police that I don't."

"I know that, but I'm asking you to think really hard about anything Lee-Ann might have said about the guy." I took a bite of doughnut and she did the same. We chewed in unison while I waited for a reply.

"She was really close-mouthed about her love life," Esperanza said after washing down the doughnut morsel with another sip of coffee. "I'm pretty sure the guy was married. I think she met him last year when she was the reigning Klondike Kate and he was with the Vulcans."

"You mean he was in last year's Vulcan Krewe?"

"I think so." She took another bite, a big one.

"So there's eight more possible suspects," I said. "But at least their names are available in our files. Do you know anything else about him?"

She swallowed more coffee. "Don't tell the cops this, but apparently the guy thinks Toni and I know who he is."

"What makes you say that?"

"We both got phone calls from someone obviously using a phony voice right after Lee-Ann's pregnancy hit the news. He must be afraid that Lee-Ann had told us who she was seeing because he warned both of us that anybody who gave any names to the police would be the next dead Klondike Kate."

I had just taken a mouthful of coffee and it went down the wrong way. After choking and coughing for a couple of minutes, I managed to croak, "Did you tell Brownie about that?"

"Who?"

"Detective Brown, the homicide chief. Did you tell him about the threat?"

"Toni was afraid to, and she made me promise not to. You're not going to put that in the paper, are you?"

"No, I'm not. But it's helpful to know these things. Tell me something else. Do you know who told the police that they saw Lee-Ann going out the backdoor of O'Halloran's with a man in a Vulcan costume?"

"No. Somebody saw that?"

"That's what I've been told, but it's strictly hush-hush until the carnival's over." I took the last bite of doughnut and a sip of coffee. "Thanks for talking to me. You may have helped me move one step closer to finding the father."

Esperanza still had almost half of her doughnut in her hand. "You won't put either Toni's or my names in the paper if you find him will you?"

"Absolutely not."

Esperanza sighed and stuffed the rest of the doughnut into her mouth.

CHAPTER ELEVEN

Search and Discovery

DUMPED THE CUP CONTAINING THE last couple of swallows of coffee into a trash can and hustled back to the office.

"Did you get a name?" Don asked as I approached his desk.

"I've got my choice of eight," I said.

"What the hell are you talking about?"

"Esperanza thinks Lee-Ann was going with a member of last year's Vulcan Krewe. It's going to take time to look up the names and talk to them."

"What are you going to say to them? 'Hi, Mr. Vulcan, were you screwing the Klondike Kate who got murdered?'"

"I'll think of something a little more subtle."

"First give me a story to freshen up the online edition," Don said. "Lead with the damn funeral if that's the best you've got, and then pad it with a little background."

I whipped out the story in ten minutes and sent it to the desk. I briefly considered calling Brownie and telling him about the threats, but decided to save that tidbit to use as trade bait for something I could print. Instead, I began searching our electronic files for a story about the identity of the previous year's Vulcans. I quickly found one headlined "Carnival's Vulcan Krewe unmasked," and opened it. The names were listed, along with their ages, home towns and places of employment. There was no information as to marital status or street address.

After printing out this story, I decided to try a different approach. I went online and called up the Winter Carnival's website. Bingo! There was a list with short bios that included the wives and kiddies.

I quickly eliminated Vulcanus Rex and the Prince of Soot as potential lovers because of their ages. Both were in their sixties, and I couldn't imagine a lusty young woman like Lee-Ann bedding down with either of them. I put the Count of Ashes as low priority because he was single and all three of Lee-Ann's close friends were convinced that her lover was married. That left five married men in the twenty-five to forty age range on my list to be contacted.

"Don tells me I'm going to have eight guys chasing me," Al said. He had sneaked up behind me and was looking over my shoulder at the computer monitor.

"I've got it down to five," I said. "And you can race them one at a time. Are you in condition to start running in fifteen minutes?"

"Are you kidding? The only thing in condition is my hair because I accidentally washed it with conditioner instead of shampoo this morning."

"If it's any consolation, I'll be running right alongside you."

"Like hell you will. You'll be at least five yards behind me so they knock you down first."

"How ironic if I'm knocked down by the man who knocked up the murder victim," I said. "I want to start with the Duke of Klinker because he works right downtown in the hockey team's office."

"Let's hope he doesn't stick it to us if he gets mad," Al said.

"We'll just have to get the puck out of there as fast as we can."

"So what are you going to say to this hockey guy?" Al asked. "Are you going ask him how many times he scored?"

"That's not my goal," I said. "These guys all knew Lee-Ann from last year's carnival. I'm going to tell them that I'm interviewing a lot of Winter Carnival participants for a roundup story prior to her funeral. I'll ask for their reaction to her murder and see what kind of response I get."

"And I'm shooting their pictures while they're punching you in the nose."

"Oh, come on. It'll be harmless, like those silly man-on-the-street interviews where you ask six people what they do for April Fool's Day and run their dopy answers with their pix."

"And you want us to start now?"

"I do. And, more important, Don wants us to."

"I'll get my camera and goalie mask and we can go see the hockey guy," Al said.

The hockey guy we were going to see was Thor Lundquist, age thirty-four, who lived in White Bear Lake, a northern suburb. According to his bio, Lundquist had a wife and two sons, and was very active in youth athletic programs. The Minnesota Wild office was only a few blocks from Lee-Ann's apartment, which gave Lundquist easy access if he also chose to be very active in adult bedroom athletic programs.

Thor Lundquist did not look pleased to see us when the receptionist led us into his office, which wasn't much bigger than a hockey goal. As I'd suspected from the name, he was all Swede, with pale blue eyes and hair so blond that it was almost white. He was also six feet tall and muscled like a hockey defenseman, the kind of man who would attract a large woman and also have the strength to strangle her.

Lundquist did not rise to greet us. Neither did he invite either of us to be seated in the only chair facing his desk.

"We didn't mean to catch you by surprise, Mr. Lundquist," I lied. "Our boss sprung this assignment on us very suddenly and we didn't have time to schedule formal meetings." Then I explained why we were there and asked the key question.

"My reaction?" Lundquist said. "Jesus, my reaction is pure horror. As I remember Lee-Ann, she was a wonderful Klondike Kate. Full of life and lots of fun to be with. It's a terrible thing to lose a woman like that."

I wondered exactly how much fun she'd been when he was with her, but his answer was direct and sincere, and his eyes never wavered from mine. I was inclined to give Lundquist an "I" for innocent, with a notation that he was both physically and geographically eligible for an affair with Lee-Ann.

"When's this story going to be printed?" he asked while Al was shooting a couple of photos.

"Thursday morning," I said. "The day of the funeral." I almost believed it myself.

"Good luck with it," he said. "You should get plenty of comments. Lee-Ann had a lot of friends connected with the carnival."

"Any who were particularly close?" I asked.

"I have no idea," Lundquist said. "Probably some of the other past Klondike Kates would be the closest. They seem to hang together like bananas in a bunch."

I wondered if I dared push my luck by asking if there was anyone in his Krewe with whom she seemed especially chummy. I decided to hold off, fearing it would alert him to what I was really after and prompt him to call his Krewe mates with a warning. We simply thanked Lundquist and left.

"So they're like bananas in a bunch, huh?" Al said when we were back out where the temperature was ten below zero.

"The group with appeal," I said.

"Apparently somebody was stalking one of them."

After that, we walked in silence for several minutes until Al asked, "What's next on the agenda?"

I looked at my watch and said, "Lunch."

"I'll buy that," Al said.

"Great. Let's go some place expensive."

"I didn't mean that literally."

"That figures," I said.

"WHERE'S OUR NEXT TARGET?" Al asked after draining his third cup of coffee.

"Actually, it is Target," I said. "Last year's Count Embrious manages one of the departments at the Target superstore on University Avenue."

The man we saw there was Dustin Wright, age thirty-one, who lived in South St. Paul with his wife and one daughter, and reportedly was "active in community affairs." Could he also be active in extra-marital affairs?

It seemed that interview would yield nothing of interest until Wright dropped the tidbit that Ted Carlson, the Vulcans manager, was one of the most active "party animals" among former Vulcans.

"Is he hitting on the women at those parties?" Al said.

"Oh, yeah, big time," Wright said. "But, hey, I'd better shut up. You won't tell Ted I was bad-mouthing him, will you?"

"No way," I said. "Al took his shots and we left, convinced that Wright had nothing to do with Lee-Ann's demise.

Our next stop was the 3M plant at the eastern edge of the city, to question chemist Donald Kryzak, the erstwhile Grand Duke Fertilious. Kryzak turned out to be short in stature (maybe five-five wearing shoes) and short of useful information.

However, he was long on brain power. He quickly saw through our scam and told us we were wasting our time because nobody in his crew had been laying Lee-Ann.

"I'd bet my next patent on that," he said. "We're all family men, except for Peter, and I think he's gay."

Peter had been the Count of Ashes. I mentally crossed him off my list.

We had two more men to call on, but their jobs were farther away and Al's shift was ending at 3:00 p.m., so those visits would have to wait until morning.

WEDNESDAY MORNING FOUND AL and me in a staff car heading east on Highway 36 to interview George Bailey, age thirty-three, a fireman in Stillwater who had served as the previous year's Baron Hot Sparkus.

I wasn't yawning as much as I was Tuesday morning because Martha and I had gone right to sleep after the news Tuesday night.

We'd both been exhausted by the energy requirements of Number 60 on the swami's list, and agreed that Number 61 would have to wait for another night.

The meeting with Bailey was short but not sweet. He'd been warned by Kryzak that we were coming and was ready with denials about partying with the Klondike Kates or having anything beyond casual contact with Lee-Ann. Another blank page in my notebook.

Still hoping to strike pay dirt, we drove south toward Hastings, a city located south of St. Paul at the confluence of the St. Croix and Mississippi rivers. Our target there was Edward St. Claire, last year's General Flameous, whose bio said he was thirty-eight years old, had a wife and two children and worked for an automobile dealer.

"We're going to ask a car salesman to tell us the truth?" Al asked.

"And nothing but the truth," I said. "Just don't let him sell you a used gas hog."

We found the dealership on Main Street, parked in a spot marked CUSTOMER and went into the showroom, where we were greeted immediately by a man with a smile as wide as a piano keyboard. He was dressed in a red-and-green plaid sport coat, red tie, and dark-green trousers. Apparently the spirit of Christmas Past still glowed brightly in this shop.

"Welcome, gentlemen," he said. "My name is Lee and I'll be happy to help you."

"That's nice," I said. "The best way you can help us is to take us to a salesman named Edward St. Claire."

The keyboard disappeared. "Oh, I'm sorry," Lee said. "Ed isn't in today. In fact, he hasn't been in for a couple of days."

"Really? When's the last time you saw him?" I asked.

"Um, actually he was here Monday, but he went home early. I think he left right after we got done watching the breaking news on that Winter Carnival singer's autopsy."

Al and I exchanged looks with eyebrows raised. "And he hasn't been back since then?" I asked.

"I don't think so. I could check with the manager," Lee said.

"Please do," I said.

"Interesting coincidence?" Al asked, as Lee hustled away.

"I've heard that timing is everything," I said.

Chapter Twelve

Where's Eddie?

S HE THINKS HER HUSBAND RAN away with some bimbo?" Al asked when I recounted my conversation with Connie St. Claire.

"She does," I said. "But I think it's more likely he ran away after knocking off the bimbo. Think about it. He's married, has two kids and a good job and is getting some on the side from a very pretty blonde. She tells him she's pregnant, he tells her to get an abortion and she refuses. He panics, dresses up in his old Vulcan suit, strangles her in the ladies room during the hubbub at O'Halloran's and for some reason dumps the body in a conspicuous driveway. Then, when he hears that the cops are doing DNA tests to find the baby's father, he panics again and skedaddles for parts unknown."

"Makes sense to me. Have you tried it on Brownie?"

"Not my job. Let him find Connie and talk to her, and then I'll trade theories with him. Meanwhile, I have a sobber to write."

I had phoned several other participants in the previous year's Winter Carnival, including King Boreas, the Queen of Snows, a couple of snow princesses, and Vulcanus Rex. From their statements, I was cobbling together a sad story about what a great person Lee-Ann was and how bad they felt about her untimely demise.

When I finished, I sent it to Don, who said it would be a one-Kleenex tear-jerker for the touchy-feely segment of our readership. "It's sentimental crap but we need to throw them a bone every now and then," said my sensitive city editor.

Filled with pride from such high praise, I went back to my desk, where I reorganized my notes on the Klondike Kate killing, shut down my computer, and put on my coat, hat and gloves.

Martha was already home when I arrived. She greeted me with the usual hug and kisses and said, "Ready for Number 61?"

"Can we eat first?" I asked.

"That's part of the plan. You'll probably need the additional fuel."

"How do you know that? Have you been reading ahead?"

"You know what they say: Forewarned is forearmed."

"I hope I won't need four arms," I said.

"You're going to be very busy with the two you have," Martha said. "Maybe you should warm them up with some pushups while you wait for supper."

THURSDAY MORNING FOUND AL and me at the O'Dell & Son Funeral Home, trying to be inconspicuous while friends of the dead woman and her family filed in. Al stood with his arms folded and I stood with my arms hanging at my sides because the triceps were sore from excessive stress in the performance of Number 61.

Lee-Ann's parents and sister, and a woman of about eighty, stood by the casket for forty-five minutes to accept words of condolence and hugs of sympathy. Five-year-old Sarajane was not in the receiving line, nor did she join the family for the service.

The sister, Lori-Luann, kept glancing at Al and me between hugs until we decided to step up and introduce ourselves. The parents gave us stiff hellos and brief handshakes. The sister thanked us curtly for our expressions of sympathy and kept her hands at her sides. The octogenarian offered a surprisingly firm hand, smiled graciously and said she was Lee-Ann's grandmother.

"Are you the one that wrote the story in this morning's paper about how Winter Carnival people loved Lee-Ann?" she asked.

"I'm the one," I said. "Al took the pictures that went with it."

"It was wonderful," she said. "I'll treasure it the rest of my days." I could hardly wait to pass that word to Don. Sentimental crap, indeed!

We thanked grandma for her compliment and retreated to the back of the room. Once seated in the last row of chairs, I took out a pocket-size notebook and began to jot down the names of the people I recognized, including some of the past Klondike Kates, most of the former Vulcans that we'd interviewed and some of the current Winter Carnival royalty I recognized.

The family had retreated to a side room, all the mourners were seated and the organist was playing the prelude when eight men in dark suits walked in, followed by Ted Carlson.

"That's the Vulcans we rode with," Al said. "They clean up pretty good."

"And they're all here," I said. "As are most of last year's Krewe, with the notable exception of one Ed St. Claire."

"Oh, and look who else just came in."

"Morning, gentlemen," said Detective Curtis Brown as he plopped onto the chair beside me. He placed the tip of his right index finger on my shoulder and said, "You I want to talk to as soon as this is over."

The minister proclaimed the occasion as "a celebration of Lee-Ann Nordquist's life." We soon learned that this meant that a lot of people would get up and talk about what great times they'd had with the guest of honor while she was among the quick. Lori-Luann went on at length about their childhood together. Grandma told about teaching little Lee-Ann to bake cookies at Christmas. A dozen or so friends, including the three former Kates I'd interviewed, gave anecdotes that were either funny or poignant or both.

Last to speak was Kitty Catalano, who looked stunning in a form-fitting black dress and four-inch black heels as she announced that the Royal Order of Klondike Kates would be organizing a scholarship fund in Lee-Ann's name. This brought smiles and a murmur of appreciation from the crowd.

Through it all, Lee-Ann's parents sat still as stones in the front row, with their arms folded and their heads hanging down.

At the end, as the organist played "Amazing Grace," Lori-Luann helped her mother rise, and supported her with an arm and a shoulder as they followed the pallbearers up the aisle and out of the church. The father walked behind them, his eyes still cast downward, acknowledging no one as he passed.

"You're not going to the cemetery are you?" Brownie asked. Al slid past us and hurried out to get a shot of the crowd on the funeral home steps as the pallbearers slid the casket into the hearse.

"No, we don't need to report on that," I said. "Besides, it's ten below again this morning."

"Yeah, I wish the damn Winter Carnival would end so the weather would warm up," Brownie said.

"Me, too. But you're not here to talk about the weather."

"How very perceptive you are. I came because you can sometimes learn a lot by checking out who attends a murder victim's funeral. Finding you here is a bonus."

"That's the nicest thing you've ever said to me."

"Treasure it," Brownie said. "It might be the only nice thing I ever say. What I want to know is what Connie St. Claire said to you."

I recapped my conversation with Connie as we walked together to the front hall of the funeral home. "Does that square with what she told you?" I asked, assuming that he had questioned the woman.

"When we got to the house late yesterday afternoon it was empty. Neighbor lady said Connie came home just after the kids got home from school, and they all got in the car and drove off. We put a watch on the house and they still haven't come home."

"Why do you suppose she did that?" I asked.

"Maybe she did know who her hubby was banging," Brownie said. "And my guess is that she doesn't want to talk to us about what happened to the bangee last week."

"So, where does that leave me for tomorrow morning's story?" I asked. "Can I say you're looking for a person or persons of interest?"

"You can. Just don't say who. And don't mention the Vulcan connection until after the big battle Saturday night."

"Do I get an exclusive on that in return for being a good boy all this time?"

"I'll let your competition read all about it in the *Daily Dispatch* before I talk about it officially. Have a good day, Mitch." Having made my day substantially better, he turned and made a quick exit.

Back at the office, I wrote a story that described the size and makeup of the funeral crowd, quoted a couple of the more poignant anecdotes and mentioned the proposed Klondike Kate scholarship. Don played it on the local front, along with Al's photo of Lee-Ann's family huddled on the front steps of the funeral home, a package no reader with a heart could possibly pass by.

I was starting to write a sidebar about the missing anonymous person of interest when Kitty Catalano appeared at my side. Her coat was unbuttoned, revealing the same form-fitting black dress she'd worn at the funeral, but I noticed that she had replaced the four-inch heels with the more comfortable red boots. She carried a large manila envelope in her right hand.

"I saw you at the funeral taking notes," Kitty said. "I thought I'd bring you the outline of the scholarship fund that the Kates are setting up." She offered the envelope, and I stood up, took the offering and laid it on my desk.

"That's a very nice gesture," I said. "Who can apply for this scholarship?"

"It's for young people who want to go into the performing arts. Music, acting, TV news, whatever."

"Very appropriate. Thanks for bringing this in."

"My pleasure," Kitty said. She took half a step closer so that our noses were only inches apart and her green eyes were looking directly into mine, and in a softer voice added, "If you have any questions about the scholarship, or want to talk about anything else at all, give me a call." She was so close that I detected the light odor of a dusky perfume, and I wanted to explore her body to locate the source.

"I might think of something I need to talk to you about," I said, with admirable self-control.

"I hope you do," she said. She winked, offered her hand for shaking and said, "Until later," as she turned away. Again, every male eye in the newsroom tracked her departure all the way to the elevator.

I took a deep breath and sat down. I sniffed my hand, which bore the scent of Kitty's perfume. There was something familiar about the smell, and I tried to recall whether someone I'd dated in the past had worn this scent. No one came to mind, and I turned to my computer and the task at hand.

In the sidebar, I wrote that St. Paul police were looking for an unnamed person of interest, who had disappeared on the day of the autopsy report. I saw this as a prelude to the next chapter in the story of Klondike Kate, in which I hoped to tell the readers whether the killer (1) had attended the funeral, (2) was the missing person of interest or (3) was someone not involved in any way with the Winter Carnival. I didn't put much stock in the third option.

CHAPTER THIRTEEN

Hail, Vulcan!

FRIDAY BEGAN ROUTINELY. When I awoke, my arms felt better because Martha and I had decided to postpone attempting Number 62 on the list until my triceps recovered from the stress of Number 61. When I went outside, I performed the car starting and scraping drill without even checking the thermometer beside the back door. On the way downtown, the radio newscaster informed me that it was "only" seventeen below.

I'd barely reached my desk when I got a call from Brownie. He said that Connie St. Claire and her children had been located at her parents' farm in Cannon Falls, about thirty miles south of Newport, but that there was no trace of Edward. I was putting together a story about the ongoing search, without naming the wife and kids, when I got a call from Karl Langford, our Capitol reporter.

"I just e-mailed you a copy of the story I sent to the desk," Karl said. "You gotta read it. Talk about an opportunistic asshole, this guy takes the prize."

"Which guy?" I asked.

"Sean Fitzpatrick."

"The gun nut pushing the bill for packing concealed weapons?"

"That's the one," Karl said. "Read the story and prepare to puke. It's slugged 'Arming Kate.'"

I called up the story and read it on my monitor. Fitzpatrick had held a press conference to proclaim that if the murdered Klondike Kate had been carrying a hidden pistol strapped to her thigh, she could have saved herself from her killer.

"When that (expletive deleted) began to strangle her, that girl could have reached under her skirt, pulled out that pistol and plugged him," Fitzpatrick had said. "That girl's unnecessary death is a perfect example of why we need this legislation."

The thought of "that girl's" family reading this piece of crap did make me queasy. This was one time I hoped nobody in that household would be reading either the online or the printed edition of our newspaper. If they learned of Fitzpatrick's blather, let it be on television rather than in the *Daily Dispatch.*

"What a sick son of a bitch," said a voice behind me. "Does he really think shooting off his mouth like that is going to win him more votes?" I turned and saw that Al had been reading over my shoulder.

"I hope he's shot himself in the foot," I said.

I'd barely finished my story when I had to update it. Brownie called again with the news that our person of interest had used his credit card at an Ohio motel just off Interstate 90 Tuesday night and again at a motel on the New York Thruway, which was also I-90, on Wednesday night.

"Nothing last night?" I asked.

"No," Brownie said. "He may have reached his destination, wherever that is. We're questioning his wife about family or friends in New York and the New England states. Have a good day."

I began to think about how the cops would handle the announcement if the person of interest was picked up before the end of the Winter Carnival. Would he be identified officially as a member of last year's Vulcan Krewe? Or would it be up to me to decide whether or not to reveal that information? If I did, Brownie might get mad and go into a protective shell. If I didn't, some other reporter, Trish Valentine perhaps, might dig it out and leave me with a face full of egg, scrambling away from an angry city editor.

"Please don't catch the bastard until Sunday morning," I said as I started to write my update.

SATURDAY WAS MY DAY OFF and Martha and I slept in until after 10:00 a.m. There was nothing on our schedule until the evening's Torchlight Parade and the ensuing Vulcan Victory Dance. We planned to attend both events, along with Al and Carol, as carnival observers, not as members of the working press. However, we also planned to keep our eyes, ears, and camera lenses open in case a clue to the killing flitted by.

Number 62 on Swami Sumi's list had left me feeling bright-eyed and bushy-tailed and eager to excel, but the woman's role had an unusual twist, and Martha's back was sore. "Next book we get will be written by a woman," she said as she sat up beside me. "I need a long, hot shower."

"Hey, I've borne the brunt of most of the off-the-wall contortions," I said. "Don't go implying that Swami Sumi is sexist."

"Well, his wife must be a hell of a lot more supple than I am." She rose slowly. As I watched her walk naked to the bathroom I noticed she didn't put the usual swing into the ass I love to stare at.

"Probably a lot younger, too," I said. Seconds later, a cold, wet washrag sailed out of the bathroom and landed on my bare belly.

The hot shower helped, and by mid-afternoon Martha's back was free of pain. We picked up Al and Carol at 4:00 p.m. and drove downtown for a pre-parade dinner at O'Halloran's, which was packed with people peeling off layers of heavy outdoor clothing, which they would reapply to their bodies when it came time to leave. The temperature outside was twelve below and falling. The forecast was for an overnight low of twenty-four below. The mercury's brief trip up to zero on Wednesday had only been a teaser.

"Better go easy on the liquids," Al said as we sat down for dinner. "If you drink too much, the cold air will have you running for a bathroom every fifteen minutes."

"Okay, I'll settle for a glass of dry wine," Carol said. She's been living with Al too long.

After a pleasant dinner, we bundled up our bodies in our warmest bundling materials and returned to the frozen realm of King Boreas to stake out a spot for watching the Torchlight Parade. The parade was to form at the eastern end of the downtown area and start moving toward us at 6:00 p.m. It would proceed west on Fifth Street for five blocks, from Sibley Street to Wabasha Street, where it would turn left and go south for one block before doubling back east on Fourth Street and dispersing.

The climactic conflict, pitting our buddies in the red Luverne against King Boreas and his blue-and-white-robed troops, was to be fought on a ten-foot-high pile of ice blocks in Rice Park, two short blocks west of Fourth Street. Although the women would be oohing and aahing over the parade, the struggle between the forces of frigidity and the warriors of warmth was the main attraction for Al and me, so we set up camp on the corner of Fourth and Wabasha, as close to the future battleground as we could get.

There was a parking ramp with a small heated lobby nearby, and we took turns, with two of us warming our noses and toeses in there, while the other two defended our claim to a narrow strip of sidewalk. Competitors for our spot grew in both number and belligerence as the time of the parade's arrival neared, and we were forced to abandon our shelter shuttle system so that all four of us could stand fast against the jabbing elbows and jostling hips of the would be usurpers of our space. Actually, the pushing and shoving had the beneficial effect of increasing our pulse rates, therefore raising our body temperatures.

"Why are so many people out here on a miserable cold night like this?" Martha asked. "Have they lost their minds?"

"They must have," Carol said. "Nobody sane stands outside when it's twenty below."

"You do realize that you're standing outside, and it's almost twenty below?" Al said.

"That's different," Carol said. "Martha and I are here to make sure you guys don't freeze your . . . well, whatever."

"Are you actually going to keep my whatevers warm?" Al asked.

"Not until later," Carol said. "If you've still got them."

I looked at Martha. "No comment," she said before I could describe the deleterious effect of subfreezing temperatures on brass monkeys.

Our conversation was saved from further deterioration by the arrival of the first unit of the Torchlight Parade. For almost an hour we watched the marching units, floats, and novelty groups do their thing while we stamped our feet, slapped our mitten-clad palms together and pressed those mittens against our cheeks to fend off facial frostbite.

King Boreas and his court rode on gaudy, lighted floats, waving regally to the peasants on the sidewalks. The Vulcans whooped it up in the Royal Chariot, with Vulcanus Rex firing off a couple of pistol shots every now and then. White-gloved baton twirlers twirled and occasionally let their silvery wands drop from unfeeling fingers. The blanket-toss girl seemed to be having the most fun as she soared high in the air, propelled by a group of muscular firefighters who provided her with a soft, safe landing after flipping her high above their heads.

I felt sorry for the marching bands, whose performances were limited to drum rolls because it was too cold to toot a trumpet or put any other musical instrument with a metal mouthpiece against moist lips. Amazingly, the number of smiles equaled the number of red noses among the parade participants as well as the spectators.

"Can anybody still move?" I asked as the last parade unit passed.

"Barely," said Al.

"This is no kind of night to be walking around barely," I said. "Put your clothes back on."

"I was going to outstrip you on the way to the battleground," Al said.

"Good idea," said Martha. "Let's run all the way to Rice Park."

"You run and get us a spot," I said. "I'll be lucky if my legs will move fast enough to walk."

"Come on," Carol said. "Last one there's a rotten snowball." She and Martha took off at a trot while Al and I followed twenty yards behind, dragging our nearly sensationless feet.

"Whose dumb idea was this?" Al asked.

"Which idea? The carnival or us watching it?" I said.

"Doesn't matter. They're both dumb."

Wondering how the women could be so damn energetic after standing in the cold for an hour, I clumped to a halt between Martha and Carol. They'd fought their way to within ten feet of the slick, frozen platform where the battle would be staged, giving Al a fine vantage point to use his camera.

Right on schedule, Boreas and his troupe ascended the stage, which glittered under a halo of colored lights. Soon we heard shouts and gunshots, and the Vulcan Krewe came roaring onto the scene. The Royal Chariot rattled to a halt and the red-clad horde poured forth, shouting, "Hail, Vulcan!"

The battle was blessedly brief. Shots rang out, the attackers swarmed onto Boreas's icy stronghold, the King of the Snows was deposed and Vulcanus Rex stood unmasked atop the highest ice block with his arms thrust skyward in triumph.

Shouts of, "Hail, Vulcan!" continued to echo through the park and the crowd began to thin as people started toward the shelter of their cars, apartments, or favorite bars. Our quartet made straight for the Crowne Plaza, where the Vulcan Victory Dance would soon get under way. Behind us, fireworks exploded above the towering Landmark Center in a carnival-ending shower of light and sound.

"Want to watch?" asked Martha, pausing and pointing toward a burst of color in the sky.

"Fireworks are for the Fourth of July," I said. "It's too damn cold to watch."

"My thought, exactly," said Al. "I'll wait for the replay on Harriet Island next summer."

"What a couple of sissies," said Carol, whose forebears were Norwegian. But she kept walking, and we joined the crowd squeezing through the hotel door into the blessed warmth of the lobby.

"The dance will be anti-climax after the battle between Boreas and Vulcan," Al said. "You might have to poke me to keep me awake. I bet I can fall asleep waltzing after being out in the cold all that time."

Little did any of us imagine what the wake-up call would be.

CHAPTER FOURTEEN

A Screeching Halt

NOT BEING MUCH OF A DANCER, I spent a major portion of the evening acting like a reporter—watching people and talking to some of the Winter Carnival folks I'd met. Martha would drag me onto the floor for a dance, and I'd escape for the next two or three. Al would take off shooting pictures of the action when he could get away from Carol for a few minutes.

"Does your husband ever stop taking pictures?" Martha asked Carol during one of Al's photo runs.

"No, he just keeps going," Carol said. "Like that bunny in the flashlight battery commercials."

Numerous men wearing Vulcan costumes, some unmasked and some still wearing the helmets and big dark goggles, were scattered through the crowd. In their red running suits, they stood out like a flock of cardinals in a grove of leafless trees. Dozens of costumed Boreas supporters, and a half-dozen women in Klondike Kate attire also circulated through the revelers. Among the latter who visited our table were Esperanza de LaTrille and Toni Erickson.

"Quite a party," I said after introducing them to Martha and Carol. "I've never come to one of these before."

"What made you come to this one?" Toni asked. "Are you writing about it?"

"Actually, I'm off duty," I said. "But riding with the Vulcans and writing about Lee-Ann triggered my curiosity."

"Do you think the bastard who killed Lee-Ann is here?" Esperanza asked.

"Not really," I said. "I think the killer has left Minnesota."

Esperanza's dark eyes opened wide. "You know who it is?" she asked.

"The police are searching for a suspect who disappeared after the autopsy report came out."

"Who are they hunting for? Who?" Toni asked.

"I can't tell you."

"Is it somebody from the carnival?" Esperanza asked.

"Sorry," I said. "That's all I can tell you for now or my police source will stop talking to me."

"We'll never tell anybody," Toni said.

"Oh, sure you won't," I said. "And the sun will never rise in the east and the snow will never melt."

"I'll bet I know who it is," Toni said. "Come on with me, Esperanza. I'll whisper it in your ear."

They hurried away and our partners hauled Al and me onto the dance floor. When we returned to the table, a masked Vulcan was sitting in the chair I'd been using. He rose, offered me the chair and said, "Hail, Vulcan!" I recognized the voice.

"Hello, Ted," I said. "All dressed up in that suit again."

"Special occasion," Carlson said. "Then it goes back into the closet until next year's carnival."

"There seem to be a lot of those suits around tonight," Al said. He slipped his camera out of the case and took a quick shot of Carlson, who tried too late to cover his face with his hands. "Don't be shy," Al said, and the camera flashed again.

"I really don't need that," Carlson said. "Anyhow, I saw you folks sitting here talking to a couple of Klondike Kates and thought I'd come by and say hello. Do you boys have anything new on the murder?" Oh, goody, we were boys again.

"Nothing the police are talking about," I said. This twerp had no need to know that they were pursuing one of his own until he read it in the paper.

"Didn't that one Kate say she thought she knew who the killer is?" Martha asked.

"She did?" Carlson said.

"She was just blowing smoke," I said. "I think everybody has a favorite suspect."

"Who's yours?" Carlson asked.

"Sorry, but I'm paid to report facts, not rumors or opinions," I said.

"But you must have a guess." This guy was becoming a pain in the ass.

"It's you," I said with a big, wide smile. "You dressed up in that outfit and went mad under the full moon last Thursday night."

Carlson took a quick step back. "That's not funny," he said. "You've got a really sick sense of humor." He spun and walked away at double time.

"That wasn't very nice," Martha said.

"In case you hadn't noticed, he was getting on my nerves," I said. "I thought that would shut him up, but I didn't think it would send him off in a huff."

The next person to visit our table was even more obnoxious. It was Sean Fitzpatrick, the gun-toting leader of LEGO, dressed in a tuxedo with tails. "Hey, guys, how're they hangin'?" he said as he approached.

"What do you say, Tex?" Al said. "I see you're all dressed up fit to kill. I just hope you don't."

"Who might these lovely ladies be?" Fitzpatrick asked.

"This lovely blonde is my wife, Carol, and this gorgeous lady is Mitch's friend, Martha," Al said.

Fitzpatrick bowed as low as a man with a bulging beer belly could bow while wrapped in a too-tight cummerbund. "Pleased to meet you, ladies," he said. "And I ain't plannin' on killin' nobody, Al. We had enough of that last week, and like I said to your Capitol reporter, that could've been avoided if—"

I cut him off. "I don't want to hear it. We're here to dance and laugh and have a good time, not talk about hiding guns in your underwear."

"Oh, Christ, nobody said nothin' about carryin' a gun in your underwear," Fitzpatrick said. "But, okay, we won't talk guns at all."

And we didn't. We talked briefly about the music, how much fun people were having and how noisy it was in the room. When Fitzpatrick asked if there was anything new on the murder, I said there wasn't and he left, after bowing again to the ladies.

"Lucky he didn't split those pants when he bowed," Al said. "They're mighty tight across the ass."

"That would have given you the picture of the week," I said. "I can see the cutline now. 'The bottom line on hidden guns.'"

"How about, 'Open season on assholes'?"

"Please, Mr. Jeffrey, this is a family newspaper."

Our fortune improved with the next visitor. It was Kitty Catalano, wearing a low-cut, purple dress that clung to every curve of her body and ended well above the middle of her thighs. Her dark hair was flowing around her bare shoulders, and I smelled that aphrodisiacal perfume again as she bent over me and grasped my hand. We almost bumped heads as I struggled up from the chair, and her hand stayed clasped in mine as I introduced her to Martha and Carol.

"I'm so glad you're all here," Kitty said. "Isn't it a great way to end the Winter Carnival?"

"It seems almost too great, considering the way the carnival started," Martha said.

"You mean poor Lee-Ann?" Kitty said. "I know we're all still grieving for her, but she'd want us to go on with the show. She was that kind of person."

"A real trouper," I said.

"She was," Kitty said. "All the Klondike Kates are. Well, it's been nice meeting all of you. And, Mitch, remember you can call me any time about any thing." She finally released my hand and drifted away on those long, long legs.

"Lady Longlegs seems to be very well acquainted with you," Martha said when I sat down beside her again.

"She's just a news source," I said.

"Do all your news sources hold your hand the whole time they're talking to you?" Martha asked.

"Only the really hot ones," I said. "But I always stay cool."

At the insistence of Martha and Carol, we danced again, and Martha clung so close that we were almost a single body on the floor. After the waltz, or whatever it was, Al and I went in search of the recently victorious Vulcanus Rex to congratulate him on his triumph over King Boreas. We found him at the bar, hoisting a tall glass of amber liquid with lots of foam on top. The big man looked as imposing unmasked as he had in the helmet and goggles.

"Ah, my part-time Vulcans," he said in a voice loud enough to be heard easily above the 100-decibel din. "I was hoping that you guys would be here. You did such a good job on that Sunday piece that I was going to hold a knighting ceremony if I saw you. My name is George, by the way. George Griswold. Griswold Plumbing and Heating. You must have seen our sign out on Payne Avenue." He put down the beer and held out both hands. I grabbed the right one and Al took the left.

"Thanks for the compliment, but you don't have to knight us," I said.

"Oh, but you deserve knighthood," he said, letting go of our hands and reclaiming the beer. "Even if you were a pain in the ass with all those questions about where the guys were when that blondie Kate got killed. I've got the certificates up in our dressing room. I'll go get them and we'll do the ceremony in front of God and everybody here at this party."

"Couldn't you just put them in an envelope and mail them to the paper?" Al asked. "We don't need all that fuss."

"No way," Griswold roared. "As the reigning Vulcanus Rex, I'm going to do this right." He lifted the glass, chugged the beer and took off to get the certificates.

"Should we disappear?" Al asked as we walked back to our table.

"That would be too rude," I said. "I think we're stuck with a public induction into the Fire King's round table."

"This isn't what I had in mind when I hoped for a hot time here tonight."

We explained what was happening to Carol and Martha, and Martha suggested that she and Carol go to the ladies' room when Vulcan reappeared.

"No, you don't," I said. "This is our day to be a knight, and you two are going to be part of the show."

"That's right," Al said to Carol. "You married me for better or for worse, and knight and day you are the one."

"We're also married in sickness and in health," Carol said. "And this is definitely making me ill."

I saw Griswold, Vulcanus Rex, bound onto the bandstand with two rolled up pieces of paper in one hand. When the music stopped, he grabbed the microphone.

"Ladies and gentlemen, we have a very special ceremony to perform at this time," Griswold said. "We are about to bestow Fire King Knighthood on two honorable gentlemen of the local press. Please come forward, Mr. Mitchell and Mr. Jeffrey, and bring your lovely ladies with you."

Hand-in-hand, the four of us marched forward and stepped up onto the platform. The current Vulcan Krewe formed a semi-circle around us and Vulcanus Rex told Al and me to kneel.

His long, silver sword went first onto my head. "Warren Mitchell, I bestow upon thee the title of Sir Sizzling Storyteller and present you with this certificate of Fire King Knighthood." He handed me the scroll and I thanked him.

Next he placed his sword on Al's head. "Alan Jeffrey, I bestow upon thee the title of Sir Flaming Photographer and present you with this certificate of Fire King Knighthood." Al took the scroll and thanked him. "You may both rise."

We got to our feet amid a crescendo of applause from the crowd, and as we smiled and waved in response we were each treated to a smear of facial grease by two quick-moving members of the Krewe. Carol and Martha were laughing and pointing at the black Vs on our cheeks when they simultaneously received matching decorations.

We waded through the congratulatory crowd toward our table, receiving quick hand shakes and pats on the back all along the way. As we passed Toni and Esperanza, they grabbed Al and me and kissed us on the unmarked cheeks. We responded by rubbing a bit of grease onto their faces, and they went away giggling like teenagers.

"I got that shot for posterity," said a voice on my other side. There stood *Daily Dispatch* photographer Sylvan "Sully" Romanov with a camera in his hand and a grin on his face. "Don will love seeing you kissing Klondike Kate."

"Klondike Kate was kissing me," I said. "Are you shooting this chaos?"

"Yup. Me and Corinne Ramey. I'm showing her the ropes." Corinne was a new reporter who'd joined the staff just in time to get the assignment nobody wanted—covering the Saturday night Winter Carnival events.

"I hope you got shots of our knighthood ceremony," Al said.

"I did," Sully said. "But Klondike Kate smooching Mitch has much more human interest. I'll bet Don picks that one over the knighting thing."

"Lucky me," I said.

"Hey, Sully said you're of interest to humans," Al said. "In your case, that's quite a compliment."

"See you around," Sully said. "I've got to corral Corinne and head back to the office so we can get this crap, uh, this historic information, into the Sunday paper. Nighty, night, guys." And off he went, in search of the roving reporter.

"Guess that leaves us to record any further historic happenings," Al said.

"Guess so," I said. "Even the TV cameras have bailed out. I'm kind of disappointed that Trish Valentine wasn't reporting live on our becoming knights of the Fire King's domain."

Four long stem glasses of champagne stood waiting for us on our table, so we clinked them together and my three companions drank theirs while I continued to hold mine high.

"Mustn't let yours go to waste," Al said when he'd finished his. He grabbed my glass and poured it down the hatch.

"Waste not, want not, Sir Flaming Photographer," I said.

"I wasn't hot for that title, but I've been called more inflammatory things than that," Al said. He picked up his camera and went off to shoot more pictures of the people in the crowd.

Al had returned, the band had taken a break and the crowd noise had dwindled from a roar to a murmur when Carol said it was time for us to go home. We all stood up, put on our hats and coats and started toward the nearest ballroom exit, which had been opened to let some of the heat from the crowd dissipate into the hall.

I was about to say it had been a perfect evening when the air was rent by a woman's scream that would have instantly transformed a quart of milk into a carton of cottage cheese.

CHAPTER FIFTEEN

A Shot in the Dark

THE SCREAM CAME FROM OUTSIDE THE BALLROOM, in the direction of the restrooms across the hall. Because we were near an open door, the four of us beat the pell-mell rush of bodies out of the ballroom, and we were in the hall before knots of frantic people clogged all the exits.

We saw a flash of red disappear through a door beneath a lighted exit sign, and two women wearing Klondike Kate costumes emerge from the ladies room. One of them fell to her knees and leaned forward, pressing her forehead against the carpet. The other one knelt beside her and put an arm around her shoulders.

A couple of men dressed as members of King Boreas's royal family dashed out through the exit in pursuit of the red streak. They were followed by a waddling fat man in a tuxedo shouting, "I'll nail the fucker!" Al and I raced toward the exit while Carol and Martha ran to help the two women on the floor.

We'd just gone out the door and felt the shock of the outside air when we heard a muffled bang, followed by a man shouting, "Oh, shit! Oh, my god! Oh, son of a bitch!" Hobbling toward us in the dim light of the alley was the fat man in the tux. He was supported on each side by a Boreas royal family member.

Al opened the door for the trio, and we followed them in. The fat man was Sean Fitzpatrick, who was moaning in pain between curse words. In his right hand, he clutched the small pistol he'd shown us at the *Daily Dispatch*.

A dark-red stain was spreading across the top of his right shoe.

"My god, Tex, did you shoot yourself in the foot?" Al asked.

"Oh, Christ, it hurts like a son of a bitch," Fitzpatrick said. "Somebody call 911."

"What the hell were you doing?" I asked.

"I was gonna plug the bastard that ran out the door, but the damn gun went off before I got it out of my leg holster." Someone dragged up a chair from the ballroom and he plopped onto it.

"You were carrying a gun hidden in a leg holster in the ballroom?" I asked.

"I was gonna have a press conference Monday and say how easy I got it in and how harmless it was," Fitzpatrick said. "It was a subtle way of provin' my point."

"Subtle?" Al said. "That was about as subtle as a fart during the silent prayer."

"Has anybody called 911?" Fitzpatrick wailed.

"They've been called. You'd better get that shoe off," said one of the Boreas court members who had helped Fitzpatrick after the shot.

Fitzpatrick tried to bend down, but his belly got in the way so he couldn't reach his foot. The other Boreas court member knelt, pulled his white costume gloves from his pocket, put them on and went to work untying the bloody shoe. When he finished, he looked up at Sean and said, "We'd have caught that guy if you hadn't shot yourself."

More people crowded around the wounded warrior, so Al and I turned our attention to the woman we'd seen fall to the floor. By this time, she also had been helped onto a chair, but she was near hysteria as a circle of women tried to calm her. When she raised her head to speak to one of her comforters, I saw that it was Toni Erickson.

Martha saw us and stepped away from the circle, which included Esperanza, Angela Rinaldi, and two others in Klondike Kate attire.

"Did she say what happened?" I asked.

"She keeps saying that a Vulcan tried to kill her," Martha said. "She's so upset that we can't get any more than that."

"That was the red we saw go out the back door," Al said. "How'd she get away from him?"

"I don't know," Martha said. "The Klondike Kate in the yellow dress was with her. Maybe she helped. I'll see if she'll come over and talk to you guys."

After a brief, low-volume conversation, the Kate in the yellow dress detached herself from the circle and came to us. "Are you the reporter I talked to about Lee-Ann?" she asked in a booming tenor voice. I said I was, and she said her name was Hillary Howard. Big surprise.

"What happened in the ladies' room?" I asked.

"I was in a stall, you know, doing my thing, when I heard a scuffle out by the sinks," she said. "I quick pulled everything together and stepped out. There was Toni and a Vulcan. He had something around her neck and she was fighting and trying to tear it off. I yelled at the guy and picked up the first thing I saw, which was one of those metal boxes the hand towels are in, and bopped him on the head with it. He let go of Toni and ran out. I started to chase him, but Toni was half strangled and scared out of her mind, so I had to help her."

"Did you see the Vulcan's face?" I asked.

"No, I couldn't see anything," Hillary said. "He was wearing his helmet and goggles and greasepaint."

"Looks like she's calmed down some," Al said. "She knows you, Mitch. Maybe you can talk to her."

I approached Toni, who sat quietly with her head down, and knelt in front of her. "Toni, it's Mitch from the paper," I said in a stage whisper. "You know, the guy you've been talking to."

She looked up into my eyes. Her cheeks were wet with tears and the spot of grease she'd acquired when she kissed me had become a black streak down the right side of her face. Her eyes were rimmed in red and open a little too far.

"A Vulcan," she said. "He tried to kill me."

"Tell me what happened," I whispered.

"I was washing my hands at the sink and I saw this red thing in the mirror coming up behind me. He must have been hiding in a stall. I tried to turn around and fight him, but he got something around my throat and pulled it tight. I got my hand loose and hit him in the nuts like you're supposed to do but it didn't seem to hurt him. He must have been wearing a cup or something, I don't know. Then I tried to pull the thing off my throat because I couldn't breathe and, thank God, Hillary came out of the stall and hit him with the towel holder and he ran out and I screamed and the next thing I knew I was on the floor in the hall. Did he get away?"

"He did, so far," I said. "The police are on the way to look for him."

"Why would some Vulcan try to kill me?"

"Could have been the same one who killed Lee-Ann."

"You think he's some kind of crazy, trying to kill all us Klondike Kates?"

"I don't know," I said. I felt a tap on the shoulder, and looked up to see a middle-aged man leaning over me.

"I'm a doctor," he said. "I'd like to look at the woman who was attacked."

"Sure," I said to him. To Toni I said, "You take it easy now. There's a doctor here to see you."

I rose and saw two EMTs and a couple of cops attending to Sean Fitzpatrick. One male EMT was on his knees removing Fitzpatrick's blood-soaked sock. The female EMT was trying to take his pulse while he continued to moan in pain. One of the cops had taken the pistol out of Fitzpatrick's hand and was bagging it in plastic. The other was shaking his head in disbelief.

"Lucky Tex was wearing the holster down low," Al said. "If he'd had it up on his hip he might have shot off something vital."

"Oh, thanks for painting that picture," I said. "Now I'll think of that every time he greets me with 'how're they hangin'.'"

"This kind of screws up our theory about Lee-Ann's murder, doesn't it?" Al said.

"You're right. Unless the missing Mr. St. Claire flew back from New York today, he can't be the Klondike Kate killer."

"So why'd he run away?"

"Your guess is as good as mine."

CHAPTER SIXTEEN

Quarantined

THE HALL WAS SUDDENLY SWARMING with policemen, both uniformed and plain clothed. One of the suits was yelling through a bullhorn, ordering everyone who wasn't a doctor or an EMT to return to the ballroom and find a seat. "Nobody leaves this hotel until we tell you to," he said.

Al had shot pictures of the activity around Fitzpatrick and Toni, and I wanted to get to the office and write a story. We made a move toward the door through which the villainous Vulcan had fled, but we were stopped by Detective Mike Reilly, who was a self-important martinet and not one of our favorite officers.

"I might have known you two would be right in the thick of any incident," Reilly said. "Get your butts back into the ballroom right now."

"We've got a story to write and photos to process," I said. "We've got less than an hour until deadline."

"And I've got a shit load of witnesses to talk to, including you," Reilly said. "Are you gonna cooperate or do I have to cuff you?"

We cooperated. Al couldn't transmit his pix because we didn't have access to a computer, but I found a reasonably quiet corner and called the desk on my cell phone. I explained to Gordon Holmberg, the Sunday city editor, that I had a great story about an attempted murder and Al had pix of the intended victim, but we were stuck in the ballroom until further notice. "I can dictate the story to somebody," I said. "And maybe somebody can come over here, slip in and get Al's camera."

Holmberg said he'd send a courier for the camera and switch me to a reporter for my story. Newspapers used to have skilled rewrite editors who could be trusted to handle a story on the phone. However, rewriters have gone the way of the dodo bird, so I found myself talking to Corinne Ramey, who became very upset that she'd left before the action. I calmed her down and dictated a report on the attempted strangulation, complete with commas, periods, and paragraph breaks. You can't be too careful when you're dealing with a kid just out of journalism school.

Five plain-clothes cops, directed by Reilly, circulated through the crowd, asking for a brief statement on what each person had seen and heard, taking names, addresses, and phone numbers as they went.

Reilly herded all the costumed Vulcans into one area and ordered those wearing hats and goggles to remove them. He took their names, addresses and phone numbers, and said that homicide detectives would be talking to each of them. "One of you Vulcans is missing, and I want to find out which one it is and what any of you know about him," Reilly said.

"You know who I don't see in that group of Vulcans?" Al whispered to me.

"Well, you probably don't see the killer because he ran out the back door," I said.

"I also don't see the hotshot PR man who talked to us tonight. What's his name? Ted something."

"Carlson," I said. I took a couple of steps closer to the group of Vulcans and scanned the faces. "I don't see him, either."

"Think we should tell Reilly?"

"What's Reilly ever done for us? I'll call Brownie first thing in the morning."

"Will Brownie be working on Sunday?"

"I bet he'll be working this Sunday," I said. "In fact, if the attempted murder had been successful, he'd be here right now."

Our attention was turned to some loud voices at one of the exits to the hall. After a moment, the uniformed cop guarding that door motioned for us to join him. Waiting outside the door was

Sully. "They sent me after your camera," he said. "This fine officer was kind enough to let me get this close to the crime scene."

Al passed his camera over the yellow plastic tape stretched across the opening, and Sully took it and waved goodbye.

"Wonder how much the bribe was," Al said as we walked back to join the women.

"Sully can put it on his expense account," I said.

"Sully knows that my crime scene shots will knock his routine crap out of the paper. I hope he doesn't delete everything in my camera on his way back to the office."

"That'd be a very negative response to your fine photo work."

"Speaking of response, I wonder what the cops have done with the intended murder victim," Al said.

"I'll see if I can find out," I said. I spotted Detective Aaron Goldberg, who I knew had a better attitude than Reilly, and approached him. He said that Toni had been taken to Regions Hospital for an examination and whatever treatment might be necessary. He also said that a leather thong that was presumed to be the attacker's weapon had been found on the floor of the ladies' room. "We'll try to match it to the marks on her neck tomorrow, when she's calmed down," he said. "We didn't dare try to put that thing around her throat in the state she's in tonight."

After phoning that information to Corinne to add to my story, I was told by Reilly our foursome could leave the hotel. "Make sure none of you leave the area for the next couple of days," he said. "We definitely want to talk to all of you since you were first on the scene."

"We all live right here in town," Al said.

"Yeah, well probably the killer does too, and I'll bet he ain't hanging around," Reilly said.

"Have a good night, detective," I said as we put on our coats for the second time.

Reilly grunted, and I suspect that only the presence of Martha and Carol prevented him from responding with an obscene gesture.

WHEN WE FINALLY GOT HOME AT a few minutes after 1:00 a.m., Martha and I were both physically exhausted and emotionally fried. Again we postponed our attempt at Number 62 and went to sleep after some rolling and thrashing. When I awoke, she was sitting up in bed with the Sunday morning paper in her lap.

The attack on Toni was splashed across two-thirds of the front page above the fold, with my story wrapped around a three-column photo of a trio of Klondike Kates hovering over Toni, who had her head down and clasped between her hands. The story jumped to page three, where it was accompanied by a shot of the Boreas court prince untying Fitzpatrick's shoe.

"That fat bastard may have shot himself in the foot in more ways than one," I said. "Legislators who aren't in the gun lobby's tank will have a hard time voting for the concealed weapons bill after they see this picture."

"I can't believe he took a concealed weapon into that dance," Martha said.

"When it comes to Sean and guns, you can believe most anything, no matter how bizarre," I said.

"Will this story be in the out-state edition? If it is, you'd better call your mother very early today."

On Sundays I always called my widowed mother, who lived on a farm near a small town called Harmony in southeastern Minnesota. My grandmother, Sara Goodrich, better known as Grandma Goodie, lived with my mother, which dampened my enthusiasm for making these calls. Grandma Goodie was the pillar of the Methodist church and could not understand my reluctance to attend religious services of any kind. Any time she answered the phone, the major topic of conversation became the salvation of my soul.

"My story didn't make the out-state deadline," I said. "But it'll be in her Monday paper, so I'll call as soon as I think they're home from church and let her know that I did not incur bodily harm." This would be a prudent gesture, because in some of my past pursuits of knowledge and justice I had been shot, bludgeoned, stabbed and nearly drowned. I didn't want her motherly imagination to run wild.

My first call of the day, after a breakfast of French toast and bacon, was to the private number of Detective Curtis Brown. As I'd wagered, Brownie was at his desk.

"Happy Sunday," I said after the usual exchange of greetings.

"Don't tell me that you're working on Sunday," Brownie said.

"Actually, I'm not, but I'm following up on last night's little dustup in the Crowne Plaza. I have a tidbit that might be useful to you."

"I'm all ears. Tidbit away."

Actually, Brownie's ears are overly-large and stuck out at almost a ninety-degree angle, which was one of the reasons that it was hard for Al to shoot him in a flattering pose. Suppressing a snicker, I said, "When your boys counted Vulcan noses after the action, there was one nose missing that we had seen in costume and talked to earlier."

"Would you care to divulge the name behind this nose?"

"It's Carlson. Ted Carlson. You may recall that he also admitted wearing his Vulcan duds the night Lee-Ann was murdered."

"You're positive he was at the dance earlier?"

"He made a big show of coming to our table to chat us up and check out our women," I said. "He got pissed and walked away when I jokingly said that I thought he was the Klondike Kate killer."

"You've always been a bundle of laughs," Brownie said. "We've talked to Carlson before, but it's worth looking at him again. Thanks for the tidbit."

"Remember how grateful you are next time I call for an update."

"You know what? I'm starting to have memory problems. Must be my advancing age. Have a good day, Mitch."

"You, too," I said, but the line was already dead.

I put down the phone and went back to perusing the Sunday paper. In the local news section I found Corinne's Winter Carnival story surrounded by photos of the Torch Light Parade, the battle to dethrone Boreas and the Victory Dance. Sully hadn't been shut out after all.

When the clock struck 1:00, I figured the churchgoers were home, and I made my duty call to Harmony. My mother answered, and after some small talk, I told her about the previous evening's excitement.

"You didn't get mixed up in a gunfight did you?" she asked.

"No," I said. "I was strictly an observer."

"The nut with the gun didn't shoot in your direction?"

"His one and only shot was in the direction of his own foot."

"I wish you'd get a nice, quiet job in a safe place, like a bank or a lawyer's office like Martha. Anyhow, your grandmother wants to talk to you."

"Oh, God," I said. And, as expected, God became the topic when Grandma Goodie got on the phone.

"Warnie baby, did you go to church this morning?" was Grandma Goodie's opening line.

"It's twenty below," I said. "All the churches were frozen shut."

"Cold weather never closes a church," she said. "Only cold hearts shut out the church, and those hearts will find themselves in a very warm place when God calls them in the end."

"My heart is warm, Grandma. Especially for you."

"Oh, pooh! It's your soul I'm worried about, Warnie baby. You should be concerned with where it's going to spend eternity."

"I'll worry about that when eternity comes closer. I'm only forty years old."

"A person is never too young to seek redemption, Warnie baby."

I sighed, and managed to change the subject to prospects for the Minnesota Twins, who would be opening spring training in

Florida in a couple of weeks. Next to God and family, the Twins were Grandma Goodie's greatest love.

"The usual lecture?" Martha asked after I hung up.

"Of course," I said. "God's messenger on Earth never lets up on my lack of church attendance."

"You could probably catch a late mass somewhere this afternoon."

"I am not now and never have been a Catholic. And there's not a Protestant church in town with a strong enough roof for me to risk going in."

The rest of the day passed routinely until we turned on the local news at 6:00 p.m. Channel 4's lead story was about the detention in upstate New York of a Minnesota man wanted by authorities for questioning in the Klondike Kate murder case. St. Paul Police identified the man as Edward St. Claire of Newport, and said they would seek extradition if necessary.

This sent me to the phone. "Tomorrow's my day off," I told the night editor who answered my call. "Please leave Don a note saying that I want to swap for some other day, and that I'll be there in the morning."

"First time I've ever heard you volunteer to work on your day off," Martha said.

"I can't sit home and let somebody else chase this one," I said.

CHAPTER SEVENTEEN

The Missing Man

WHEN THE ALARM RANG MONDAY morning, my legs were entangled in a top sheet that had come undone while Martha and I were winding our way into position Number 62 on Swami Sumi's list. My pillow was on the floor and my head was snuggled between Martha's breasts, which was a far better resting place than any manmade object.

"Are you really going out in the cold on a day you could stay buried in this nice warm bed after I've gone to work?" Martha asked.

"I really am," I said. And I did, to the amazement of my fellow workers.

"What are you doing here?" asked John Boxwood. "Is the company threatening to lay off all non-essential reporters?"

"Some stories require the undivided attention and consummate skills of the ace of the staff," I said. "The Klondike Kate killing cannot be left to just any general assignment drone."

"Did you forget what day this is?" Al asked when he saw me at my desk.

"Quite the opposite," I said. "I remembered that it's my duty to follow the story of Klondike Kate through habitual holidays as well as hell and high water."

Naturally, my first call was to Brownie. The line was busy on my first three tries, but he picked up on the fourth and told me to hold. There was a click and I was treated to almost five minutes of sound that apparently was meant to be musical. Again I amused myself with two paper clips while I waited, but I found it impossible to twist them into a simulation of position Number 62.

"You're wondering about St. Claire, no doubt," Brownie said when he came back.

"No doubt," I said. "Where'd they find him?"

"Town in New York called Tonawanda. It's near Buffalo and Niagara Falls, but I don't think he was headed for a second honeymoon because he was all alone."

"Did he say why he took off? If last night's action is any indication, he didn't kill Lee-Ann."

"We don't have a statement about his reason for leaving, and we can't assume he's not a suspect. Last night's attacker might have been a copy cat."

"Do you really believe that?"

"It's kind of low on a scale of ten, but we can't just write off St. Claire. We know he was involved with the victim, and he did, in fact, run."

"How was he involved with Lee-Ann? Sexually?" I knew the answer, but I needed to hear Brownie say it.

"I can't comment on that at this time," Brownie said. "The chief may discuss that issue at a press briefing here at 10:00 a.m. Your desk should be getting a call about that."

"On a scale of one to ten, it's an eleven that I'll be there. Is the district attorney in the process of extraditing St. Claire?"

"He's waived it. We're sending two officers out there to escort him home. We're not saying what airline we're using or what the arrival time will be because we don't want a media circus at the airport."

"We could stake it out," I said.

"Be my guest," Brownie said. "It could be another long stake." He was gloating over a previous watch for a suspect at Minneapolis-St. Paul International Airport. Al and I spent the whole day checking airline arrivals while the cops were sneaking their man into St. Paul's Holman Field on a small chartered plane.

"Okay, what else is new? Have you talked to last night's attack victim?"

"The chief will discuss that issue at a press briefing here at 10:00 a.m."

"Do you have any idea why Toni Erickson was attacked?"

"The chief will discuss that issue at a press briefing here at 10:00 a.m."

"What about Ted Carlson?" I asked. "Have you questioned him about his whereabouts at the time of the attack last night?"

"The chief will not, I repeat, not discuss that issue at a press briefing here at 10:00 a.m. And I won't discuss it this morning, either. Have a good day, Mitch."

I didn't bother with a reply because I knew he wouldn't hear it.

I told Don I'd be going to the police station at 10:00, and he told me to take Al along. "Tell your twin to shoot somebody besides your buddy Brown with the landing-flap ears," Don added.

I'd barely returned to my desk when the phone rang. When I answered, I heard, "It's Morrie."

I choked back a scream and said, with remarkable calm, "I thought you'd found a new helper at the number I gave you." Damn it, the little pest was supposed to have transferred his troubles with the Russians and Robinson to John Robertson, Jr., at the Minneapolis paper.

"That man stopped the Russians' radar but he hasn't stopped Robinson," Morrie said. "In fact, he told me that he knows Robinson personally and that Robinson is still out to get me. You've got to write about it so he'll stop."

"What's Robinson look like? Have you got a picture we could run with my story if I write one?"

"Oh, I've never seen Robinson. I don't know if anyone has."

Why was I not surprised? "Your best bet is to stay in your apartment all day, with the shades down and the curtains closed. And don't use your phone or he'll be able to trace the call."

"Oh, jeez, I never thought of that. Do you think I should hang up right now?"

"I do," I said. And he did.

I put down the phone and cursed John Robertson, Jr., for sending Morrie back to me. Looking across the newsroom, I saw cartoonist Dave Jerome approaching double-time with a piece of paper in his hand and a grim expression on his face. "Look at this," he said when he reached my side. "Tell me what this is." He pointed to the drawing of a long-handled cane with its curved end wrapped around the neck of a fat character labeled Sean Fitzpatrick.

"That's a hook, like they used to yank people off the stage in Vaudeville if their act was too long or too putrid," I said.

"Thank you," Dave said. "That makes ten out of eleven people in this building who have identified it correctly."

"Is this a problem?"

"That . . . the new editor, Ron, is the odd man out. He looked at this cartoon and pointed to the hook and asked me what it was. When I told him, he said nobody under the age of eighty would have a clue about what it was. Like I said, I've shown it to ten other people, all of them well under eighty as far as I can tell, and they've all recognized it."

"So you're showing the sponsors of the concealed weapons bill yanking Sean Fitzpatrick offstage for his Saturday night fiasco, and Ron doesn't understand it?"

"Exactly," Dave said. "The man just does not understand cartoons." Ronald C.R. Carter, who used both of his middle initials in his byline, had been sent to us by corporate two months earlier as our new editorial page editor. This was not the first time that Dave had come out fuming after showing Ron a cartoon.

"May your ten votes prevail when Ron hears the tally," I said. "Now I have to go find out what the cops have found out from our erstwhile fugitive, Ed St. Claire. Great cartoon, by the way."

Dave grunted and headed back to Ronald C.R. Carter's office.

Chief Casey O'Malley's 10:00 a.m. press briefing brought out the usual mass of reporters and photographers from every newspaper and TV station in the Twin Cities. Trish Valentine had arrived in time to grab a front-row spot, which I assumed would please the chief because she was wearing another snug sweater. Al and I wormed our way to the second row, behind two shorter people from the Minneapolis paper.

O'Malley was accompanied by Brownie, but the chief did all the talking. "First let me say that I won't be taking any questions at the end of this briefing. Next let me say that the man who was apprehended in New York state, Mr. Edward St. Claire, a resident of Newport, is a person of interest because we have learned that he had a relationship with Ms. Lee-Ann Nordquist and he left Minnesota at a time concurrent with the coroner's report on the cause of her death. However, to categorize him as a suspect would be premature at this time.

"Obviously Mr. St. Claire had nothing to do with last night's attack on Ms. Toni Erickson in a restroom at the Crowne Plaza Hotel. We questioned Ms. Erickson about that incident this morning, and she believes the attempt on her life may have been inspired by the fact that she told several people in the crowd that she thought she knew who killed Ms. Nordquist.

"As you know, Ms. Erickson's attacker was dressed in a Vulcan costume. This lends credence to her theory about the attacker's motive because the murder victim, Ms. Nordquist, was last seen alive in the company of a man wearing a Vulcan costume."

This revelation drew a murmur of amazement from the crowd. It also blew away the exclusive item that Brownie had promised me in return for my withholding the Vulcan connection until the end of the carnival. I whispered an expletive and fixed my eyes on the homicide chief. A minute later, possibly because he felt the heat of my stare, Brownie looked my way. When he saw the expression on my face, he shrugged and looked elsewhere.

Chief O'Malley rattled on about Toni having been treated and released at Regions Hospital Sunday night, and having allowed them to match the leather thong found in the ladies room to the mark on her neck this morning. He finished with the news that Sean Fitzpatrick also had been treated at Regions and released for the wound in his foot, and that he had been charged with carrying a concealed a weapon and discharging said weapon in an unsafe manner. After leaving the hospital, Fitzpatrick had been booked and released on his own recognizance.

"Sounds like poor old Tex should have waited until they passed that law he's pushing," Al said as we left the police station. "You might say he jumped the gun."

I was too angry about having my Vulcan exclusive shot down to fire back a reply.

I'D JUST GOTTEN SETTLED AT MY DESK when phone rang. "It's Brown," he said when I answered.

"Calling with an exclusive?" I replied.

"Calling to apologize. I didn't know the chief was going to say that about the Vulcan costumes. He doesn't run his statements past me before he speaks."

"And you, of course, hadn't told him about our deal."

"What the chief doesn't know doesn't hurt him. Or me."

"Well, this time it pissed me off," I said.

"I have something else to offer as a replacement," Brownie said. "Something I've been sitting on and the chief didn't mention."

I picked up my pen and grabbed a piece of scratch paper. "And what is your exclusive offering?"

"It comes from a source that can't be named, but I'm sure you'll figure out who it is. Anyhow, this source believes that Edward St. Claire is the father of Ms. Nordquist's unborn baby."

CHAPTER EIGHTEEN

Feeling Better

MY FIRST RESPONSE TO BROWNIE was to ask if his source's initials might be Connie St. Claire.

"Like I said, my source can't be named," Brownie said. "And neither can yours. Just say yours is reliable. My anonymous source and a couple others told us Mr. St. Claire had been having sexual relations with Ms. Nordquist ever since they met last year."

"So the pregnancy could be his motive for murder," I said.

"Smart boy."

"Okay, the Lee-Ann Nordquist killing seems about to be solved. But if St. Claire did it, we're left with the question of who wearing a Vulcan costume tried to kill Toni Erickson and why."

"If you figure that one out, let me know," Brownie said. "Have a good day."

Mine had just gotten a whole lot better.

After finishing my story, with St. Claire's possible fatherhood in the lead, I decided to make a call that could further improve my day. Kitty Catalano had offered to give me additional details on the Klondike Kate scholarship or discuss anything I wanted to talk about whenever I had time. Since I had no other assignments, this looked like the perfect time to visit a lovely, long-legged lady, providing she had time.

She did. In fact, she was free for lunch and said she'd meet me anywhere but O'Halloran's or the Crowne Plaza. We agreed on a small sandwich shop a block from her office.

As if cued by the end of the Winter Carnival, the downtown temperature had soared to twenty-six above zero, making the air feel almost balmy as I walked to the restaurant. My internal temperature also soared when Kitty rose to greet me. She was dressed in the same snug white sweater and form-fitting gray slacks she'd worn the first time we met. Her dark hair swirled around her shoulders as she pushed back the chair and stepped toward me. The only thing missing from our original meeting were the red boots, which had been replaced by a pair of black heels only slightly shorter than those she'd worn at the funeral.

She surprised me with a full frontal hug—Minnesotans just don't do that—and set my right ear on fire with a breathy greeting. We took seats facing each other at a small, square table, so close that our toes collided when we stretched our legs simultaneously.

Questioning Kitty on the phone and in the office had been easy, but the hug, the ear-warming whisper and a close-up whiff of her haunting perfume had me so discombobulated that I found myself stuck for an opening line. Consequently, I sat gazing into her green eyes in silence until I became uncomfortable.

"Weather's much better, now that the carnival's over," I said at last, trying to break the ice. When at a loss for words, you can always talk about the weather in Minnesota.

"Seems like it's always that way," Kitty said. "You freeze your buns off for almost two weeks and then, when you don't have to go outside anymore, it warms up."

I wanted to say that her buns appeared to have thawed very nicely, but it seemed too early for flirtatious small talk. Instead, I said, "If we had any brains, we'd all go south in the winter and leave St. Paul to the glaciers."

Her smile would have melted those glaciers. "But then we wouldn't have a Winter Carnival, would we? And you and I wouldn't be enjoying each other's company."

"Maybe we'd meet on a beach in Key West instead." I felt like I was babbling inanities in front of this elegant woman. I was rescued by our server, who introduced herself as Maggie and asked what we wanted to drink. Kitty ordered a glass of Chablis and I asked for my usual ginger ale.

"You don't drink on the job?" she asked.

"I don't drink at all," I said. "I'm an alcoholic."

"That sucks. You mean you can't even have one teeny-weeny glass of wine?"

"I've learned the hard way that when I have one teeny-weeny glass of wine it expands into a great big gallon of booze pouring into a slobbering, snot-flying drunk."

Kitty wrinkled her nose and said, "Whatever. So, do you want to talk about the scholarship now or later?"

"Let's do it now and get it out of the way," I said.

"I like that idea. Then we can talk about more interesting things while we eat." From her handbag, she produced another press release in a Klondike Kate folder and spent all of two minutes explaining how the scholarship would be managed and who would be eligible. She passed me the folder and said, "Any questions?"

I had none. I was searching for my next line when Maggie returned with our drinks. We ordered our sandwiches, and Maggie hustled away. We hoisted our glasses, clinked them together and said, "To Klondike Kate."

This time I was ready with a question. "So, what do you do when you're not coordinating the Klondike Kates?"

"Very little," Kitty said. "Once the Winter Carnival is over, all I have to do is schedule Kates for various events during the year and make sure they get where they're supposed to be when they're supposed to be there. They do get involved in a huge number of events, and now, of course, I'll have the scholarship to deal with, but it's still a very easy job."

"I was thinking more about non-working hours when I asked that question."

"I can give you the same answer. Very little. My social life sort of revolves around the Kates and the carnival."

"No family here?" I asked.

"My family's all in Wisconsin and Illinois," Kitty said. "I grew up in Madison and graduated from UW with majors in English and theater. I taught high school English and directed the plays for a year, and moved here a couple of years ago to be with a guy, but that broke up almost as soon as I got here."

"What kind of a guy would break up with a beautiful woman like you?"

"The kind of a guy who likes to play around with more than one beautiful woman at a time. It was tough to find out that I was second fiddle, but I'm still glad I followed him to St. Paul. I like it here."

"It's a good place to live. How'd you get into the Klondike Kate competition?"

"I was working in a bank with a woman who'd auditioned the year before. She said it was a lot of fun and that I'd have a good chance of winning. It was fun, but, as you know, the judges picked Lee-Ann as number one."

"Apparently you were a gracious loser," I said. "I mean applying for the administrative job when it opened."

Kitty nodded and smiled. "I kind of fell in love with the organization during the auditions. Like I said the first time I met you, the Kates are like family. Now let's talk about something besides me. You, for instance."

I gave her a quick rundown of my life, from boyhood on the farm, to University of Minnesota graduate, to Navy flight crew, to the soul-crushing loss of wife and baby in a car crash, to the subsequent descent into the darkest depths of alcoholism, to treatment and to a job at the *Daily Dispatch*.

"Ever thought about a second marriage?" Kitty asked when I finished.

"Once," I said. "The day I was going to propose, the object of my affection told me she was going away to live with her high school sweetheart."

"Nice timing. You seem to have had a rough time with women. Anybody in the picture now?" I'd been wondering when that question would come up, and I'd been wondering how I'd answer it. I decided to be both truthful and vague.

"Right now I'm working on a relationship with a divorced woman, but we both have commitment problems," I said. "In fact, you met her Saturday night."

"Oh, sure, the gorgeous brunette," Kitty said. "I can understand your problem. I'm a little gun-shy myself after finding out that the only guy I'd ever slept with was also screwing some other woman. Not that he or anyone else has ever asked me for a commitment."

"That's surprising. Beautiful woman like you."

She actually blushed. "Thank you. Maybe someday I'll get to play first fiddle instead of second."

We steered the conversation into less personal waters, finished our sandwiches and paid the tab (with Kitty insisting on covering her own). I walked her back to her building and when we exchanged good-byes she surprised me with another hug. "If you and your friend decide you can't commit, you know my phone number," she said.

After that invitation, I went home with an interior glow and an exterior trace of Kitty's perfume remaining from the hugs. However, the inner glow began to fade when I thought back on the conversation. Why hadn't I been firm about my loyalty to Martha when Kitty asked about our relationship? Why had I left the door open to a test run with Kitty when I should have closed and locked it? Was commitment to each other our problem or was it just mine? By the time Martha came home a little more than three hours later the glow had been snuffed out by a sodden blanket of guilt.

The level of this guilt rose like a thermometer in August when Martha's keen female nostrils picked up the scent of Kitty's perfume as I welcomed her with a hug. "Have you had company this afternoon?" she asked, crinkling her nose and sniffing.

I plunged with too much fervor into a story about my business lunch with Kitty and the surprising, un-businesslike hugs. "I think she's feeling the strain of the murder of one friend and the attempted murder of another," I said.

"You sure that's all she's feeling?" Martha said.

"What else could it be?"

"Don't play dumb with me," Martha said. "You are not an unattractive man."

"Flattery will get you everywhere," I said.

Later that night, when I returned from my AA meeting and a quick ginger ale with Jayne Halvorson, Martha suggested temporarily ditching the Swami's book and making love the old-fashioned way.

Her suggestion reminded me of a song about that old-time religion that my mother used to sing when I was little kid. "It was good enough for Grandpa and it's good enough for me," I said. And it was good for both of us, long into the night.

ON TUESDAY MORNING, the temperature was again in the positive twenties, so naturally it snowed. My car was covered with a three-inch-thick white blanket, and my face took a beating from a flurry of icy flakes driven by a stiff northwest wind while I brushed off the windows and the hood.

The drive downtown was agonizingly slow because the streets had not been plowed and the traffic had churned the snow into a greasy gray mass. When I finally reached my desk, ten minutes late according to Don, my first call of the day went to Brownie. "Anything new?" I asked.

"It's snowing like a son of a bitch," Brownie said.

"If I wanted a weather report, I'd have called the Weather Bureau. What about the Klondike Kate killing?"

"Not much at this time. We questioned that Carlson character again. He said he left the dance shortly after talking to you and went home. His wife verifies that he was home with her at the time of the attack on Ms. Erickson."

"Do you think they're telling the truth?"

"I do. The wife has a nasty cold and couldn't go to the dance. He'd promised to come home early and she seemed pleased that he'd kept his promise. I also got the impression that this was a surprise."

"So, that eliminates him as the possible attacker?" I asked.

"It does," Brownie said. "Unless somebody else can put him at the dance at the time of the attack."

"Which makes that whole interrogation a non-news item. What about St. Claire?"

"Can't do much for you there either until the DNA sample comes back. We sent it to a private lab with a request to expedite. We'll have the results in a couple of days, and I'm betting there's a match."

This cock-sure attitude made sense. If Lee-Ann Nordquist was the woman with whom Connie St. Claire thought her husband was cheating, he was the most likely candidate for fatherhood. The timing of Edward St. Claire's decision to disappear, immediately upon the announcement of Lee-Ann's pregnancy, made it seem even more of a sure thing.

"Here's the way we see it," Brownie said. "Ms. Nordquist tells her married lover that she's pregnant. Married lover says go see a doctor about an abortion. Ms. Nordquist refuses to have an abortion and says she'll be needing child support. Married lover says fuck off. Ms. Nordquist says if I don't get it I'll tell your wife what we've been doing. Married lover hauls out his old Vulcan running suit, takes advantage of the mob scene at O'Halloran's, gets Ms. Nordquist off in a corner by the restrooms, twists a cord around her neck and walks out with the body like he's helping a drunk stay on two feet. But the DA won't drag this suspected married lover into court on a murder charge until we have DNA results confirming that he is the daddy. Have a good day, Mitch."

This scenario coincided with mine. I put down the phone and went to the photo department to run Brownie's recitation past Al. He agreed that everything pointed to St. Claire.

"I should have borrowed a picture of him when I was talking to his wife," I said. "She had a picture on her desk of herself looking lovey-dovey with a guy that must have been him."

"I wonder if she would've given it to you if you'd asked," Al said.

"Who said anything about asking?"

"You're thinking of the Navy way of borrowing things, known as cumshaw."

"Come see, cumshaw," I said. "Assuming we're right about St. Claire, we still don't have a handle on who tried to kill Toni Erickson. The cops think she was attacked because she was blabbing to everybody about knowing who killed Lee-Ann, but why would somebody go to that extreme in order to protect lover boy St. Claire?"

"God only knows."

"And She ain't telling."

"In other words, we haven't got a prayer," Al said.

CHAPTER NINETEEN

Square Pegs

THE ST. CLAIRE SCENARIO TOOK A HIT the following day when I was visited by a lanky, athletic-looking young man wearing a snow-flecked London Fog raincoat and black-knit hat similarly dotted with white. He seemed vaguely familiar, but I couldn't say why.

"Remember me?" he asked as he offered his hand for shaking. "I'm Tony."

"And your last name would be?" I asked as I took his hand and discovered it was wet with melted snow.

"Costello," he said. "Tony Costello. The Count of Ashes. When you rode with our Krewe, you asked me about being in O'Halloran's Bar the night Klondike Kate, Lee-Ann, got killed."

"Okay," I said. "As I recall, you blew me off and stayed far, far away for the rest of the ride."

"Orders from headquarters. The cops ordered us all not to talk to anybody, especially nosy reporters. The chief himself told us he'd toss our asses in the clink if we blabbed. Those exact words."

"That's very interesting. While the chief was telling you to stonewall the media, the head of homicide was telling me to find out everything I could while I was with you guys that day. So what brings you to my desk this morning?"

"I read your story about Eddie St. Claire being hauled in for questioning," Costello said. "And I think the cops have got the wrong guy."

"What makes you think that?" I asked.

"Have you seen Eddie? He's short. Not much taller than Lee-Ann, who was only about five-four. The guy in the Vulcan suit who walked out with her that night was a lot taller. Probably close to six feet."

"How do you know that?"

"I saw them."

That got my attention. "You're the anonymous witness?"

"That's right," he said. "The cops—a detective Brown—ordered me to keep my mouth shut about that."

"Have you told this height thing to the cops?"

"Not yet, but I will," Costello said. "I stopped here to see you on the way to the station so you won't slander Eddie anymore."

"I haven't slandered Eddie," I said. "Slander is verbal. It has to do with the spoken word. Newspapers *libel* people, they don't slander them. But my story can't be construed as libelous because I was quoting the police verbatim. You can talk to Brown about slander, but he'll tell you where to stick it."

"Jeez, you're a walking dictionary. That's a shit load more than I wanted to know about slander."

"Well, you haven't told me anywhere near what I want to know about Lee-Ann and the badass Vulcan. Tell me exactly what you saw in O'Halloran's that night." I had picked up a small tape recorder off my desk and I flipped it on to record his response.

"It's pretty much what you had in your story about the police chief saying a Vulcan was the last one to see Lee-Ann alive. I was watching Lee-Ann because I was hoping to get next to her myself. But, this Vulcan, and I don't have a clue who it was, except I'm sure it wasn't anybody from our Krewe, was cozied up with her at a table in the back, buying her drinks and shooting the shit. She was obviously feeling no pain when she got up to go to the can because she did the old zig-zag on the way.

"Anyhow, Lee-Ann was barely out of sight when the Vulcan got up and headed in the same direction. I figured he was going to the men's room."

"Let me get this straight," I said. "You were watching Lee-Ann because you wanted to be the one getting her drunk?"

"Not drunk, just mellow," Costello said. I smiled and gave what I considered to be a knowing nod, a gesture from one horny male to another. "Hey, don't give me that fisheye," Costello said. "I'm single and I thought Lee-Ann was cute."

"Okay. Sorry I interrupted. Finish your story."

"I wasn't watching for Lee-Ann to come back from her piss call because Marcus, Count Embrious, was telling a joke and I turned around to listen to it. When he finished, I looked back just in time to see the two of them, the Vulcan and Lee-Ann, go out the back door to the parking lot. It looked like he was pretty much supporting her, which didn't surprise me considering how wobbly she'd been on the way to the ladies' room."

"Do you think she might have been dead when they walked out the door?"

"That's spooky, but yeah, I do now. The bastard must have killed her back there in the ladies room, just like he went after the other girl, Toni What's-her-name, at the dance Saturday night."

"But you didn't see the Vulcan who attacked Toni?"

"No. The action was all over by the time I got through the jam-up in the ballroom door. Obviously, that wasn't Eddie, 'cause he was somewhere out in New York."

"Obviously," I said. "And you're going to tell Brown or whoever about this height differential?"

"As soon as I leave here, which I guess is now," Costello said. "Unless you got more questions."

"Not at the moment." I offered him a notepad and a ballpoint pen. "Leave me your phone number in case I have some later."

Costello accepted the pad and pen, scribbled his numbers at work and at home, apologized for accusing me of slander and went on his way to the police station, leaving me to wonder how this square peg fit into the round hole with everything else I knew.

I ran my conversation with Costello past Al in the lunchroom at noon.

"This case gets screwier all the time," Al said. "It seems like the more we find out the less we know. I was sure there were two Vulcans involved, a killer and a wannabe, but now it looks like we're back to one Vulcan. Who the devil could it be?"

"Beats hell out of me," I said.

T HE St. Claire scenario took an even bigger hit from another square peg two days later. I was shutting down my computer late Friday afternoon when my plan to leave the office was sidetracked by a call from Brownie.

"You want the bad news or the worst news?" he asked.

"Give me the worst news first," I replied.

"The worst news is that Edward St. Claire's DNA test came back, and his DNA doesn't match that of the Nordquist fetus."

"And the not as bad news?"

"We had to release him for lack of evidence, even though he's still a person of interest in the case."

"If he's not the father, why would he still be a person of interest? What would be his motive for killing Lee-Ann?"

"Jealousy. He was screwing the woman at least three times a month. Then she goes out and gets knocked up by somebody else."

This was news, although I wasn't quite sure how I'd write it. "Did he admit to screwing her at least three times a month?" I asked.

"Not at first, but he quit denying he'd been banging her regularly when we told him that we had evidence to prove it," Brownie said. "Because Mr. St. Claire is a car salesman, he belongs to a number of civic organizations in order to make contacts. These organizations meet once a month, the Kiwanis on a Tuesday, the Elks on a Wednesday and the Lions Club on a Thursday. He would tell his wife he was going to one of those meetings when his real meeting was with Ms. Nordquist in a motel up I-494 in Woodbury."

"How'd you discover that?"

"By talking to Mrs. St. Claire. It seems that the Kiwanis treasurer called the house a couple of weeks ago to remind Mr. St. Claire that he needed to pay his dues, and Mrs. St. Claire took the call. Said the treasurer told her that they hadn't seen her husband at a meeting for eight or nine months and asked if he was okay."

"I'll bet he wasn't so okay after that," I said.

"She was smart," Brownie said. "She kept her mouth shut, but the next time he left for a Kiwanis meeting she got in her car and followed him. She watched him check into the motel, then went home and dug through his old credit card bills. And guess what? She found a regular pattern of visits to that particular motel."

"The idiot used his credit card to shack up with Lee-Ann?"

"Apparently he doesn't carry much cash. Anyway, the wife was just about ready to let the shit hit the fan right when Ms. Nordquist was murdered and the coward took off. Now we have the credit card records for the motel and a list of people from the Kiwanis, Elks and Lions to talk to about Mr. St. Claire's attendance record."

"So you still think St. Claire might be the killer?"

"We can't write him off. He's still got a motive."

"What about the physical thing?" I asked. "You know, the fact that he's short and that other Vulcan, Costello, said he saw a taller man with Lee-Ann?"

"Witnesses are always making mistakes about height, weight, age, color of hair, number of arms and legs, what have you," Brownie said. "Somebody else who was there that night told us that the Vulcan hanging around Ms. Nordquist was average height, whatever the hell that is."

"So what's the official police line on all of this?"

"That Mr. St. Claire was having an affair with the victim, but that his DNA test was negative as far as being the father of her unborn child, and he has been released from custody at this time. You can dress it up anyway you want, but go easy on his poor wife. Have a good day, Mitch."

Chapter Twenty

North by Northeast

THAT NIGHT MARTHA and I dined with the Jeffrey family again. Martha had baked a pecan pie, which made her even more popular than usual with the teenagers, Kristin and Kevin. After the pie had been demolished and the adults were sipping the last of their coffee, Martha dropped a bomb not at all popular with me.

"I'm going to be away probably all next week," Martha said. "We're trying a civil case in Duluth and the lead attorney wants me to be second chair."

"Congratulations," Carol said. "That could be great experience for you."

"Take your long johns," Al said. "If you think it's cold here, wait until you feel the winter wind whipping off Lake Superior."

"Who's the lead attorney," I said. I had visions of Martha spending a week in the same hotel with an up-and-coming law office stud muffin.

"Sara Norris," Martha said. "You met her at the Christmas party."

Indeed, I had met Sara. She was slim, brunette, in her early forties, and best of all, the married mother of two teenagers.

"HOW AM I GOING TO KEEP warm while you're gone all next week?" I asked about three hours later as we were undressing for bed.

"You've always got Sherlock," Martha said.

"It ain't the same," I said, doing my best not to sound whiny.

"Sorry, sweetie, but duty calls. If the paper sent you to Duluth for a week, I'm pretty sure you'd go."

"Don would never send me that far."

"He once sent you to Martha's Vineyard, which is a heck of a lot farther."

"That was a very unpleasant special assignment," I said. "And I'll never have to go there again."

"What if I want to go there?"

"You can go with Sara Norris."

"That wouldn't be much of a honeymoon."

That froze my tongue for a moment. "Did I hear you say honeymoon?" I asked after the pause.

"That's a possibility sometime down the road, is it not?" she said. She was naked on the bed, stretched on her right side like a svelte, nubile feline, and was staring up at me with wide hazel eyes. Talk about timing.

"I possibly could be persuaded, sometime down the road," I said, dropping my under shorts to the floor and stepping out of them as briskly as if I was dancing on a bed of hot coals.

"Then don't do any more whining while I'm keeping you warm for the next couple of nights." Apparently my best effort not to sound whiny had been insufficient.

"Should I get the book and look up Number 63?"

"Let's leave the book alone until I get back from Duluth. That old time lovin' was pretty good last night."

WHEN THE ALARM WENT OFF MONDAY MORNING, I turned my head toward the bedroom window and discovered that it had become opaque during the night. The outside surface was plastered with a wind-driven layer of white. The TV weather pundits had forecast high winds and several inches of snow, and this time they were right.

I turned back toward Martha, who lay on her back to my right. "Not a nice day to fly to Duluth," I said.

"Who said anything about flying," Martha replied. "We're driving up in Sara's Subaru."

"You're driving northeast for 150 miles in this shit?"

"It's an all-wheeler. We'll be fine."

"Better wear your ski pants and snow boots. You'll probably be out shoveling."

Martha sat up and let the covers slide off her bare breasts, an erotic unveiling that always disarmed me. "You think because we're women we can't drive in a little old snowstorm?" she said.

"I didn't say anything about you being handicapped by your gender," I said. "I don't think anybody of any sex, color, or creed should be driving to Duluth today. In fact, I'd rather not be driving to downtown St. Paul." I turned away from Martha, curled into the fetal position and pulled the covers over my head. Her response was a knee applied solidly to my glutei maximi.

"Okay, weather wimp, you can lay there and suck your thumb until I'm out of the shower," Martha said. I felt the bed shake as she rose, and I sat up just in time to watch her wondrous ass disappear through the bathroom door. I sank back onto the pillow and reminded myself that a few hours ago this gorgeous woman had talked about the possibility of a honeymoon.

Such a possibility was both exciting and scary. Would I really have the guts to tie the knot officially? Maybe. Would she? Who knows?

And if we did tie the knot, would I go along with a honeymoon on Martha's Vineyard if that's what she really wanted? No way. Hawaii would be a lot more fun if Martha had her heart set on an island honeymoon.

The snow was the heavy, wet variety that stuck to everything. By the time I gave Martha her tenth and final goodbye kiss while standing outside the door to the parking lot, the trees, shrubs, and cars had been coated with at least two inches of prime snowball material. I resisted the temptation to scoop up a handful, scrunch it into a sphere and fire it at Martha's back as she slogged toward Sara's Subaru. When she reached the car, I waved and turned to go indoors. A solid whack between the shoulder blades told me that Martha had been unable to squelch the same devilish desire before getting into the car.

After a long session of brushing and scraping, I got the windows and lights of my Civic sufficiently uncovered to make the trip downtown. Thanks to the Weather Bureau's forewarning, the plows had been out and the streets were in what Minnesotans call "good winter driving conditions," with the emphasis always on "winter." My biggest problem was keeping the windshield clear because the heavy, wet flakes glued themselves to the glass.

Martha had agreed to keep me posted on the progress of the Subaru at regular intervals, and her first call came moments after I shook the snow off my storm coat and hung it on the rack in the newsroom. They were on I-35 north, creeping along in heavy, slow-moving traffic.

I'd no sooner wished Martha better luck and hung up than the phone rang again. When I picked it up, I heard the dreaded voice of Morrie.

"The Russians have got their radar aimed at my building and they're bombarding me with snow," he said. "You've got to write about it and stop them."

"It's snowing everywhere, not just on your building," I said. "The storm is all over the state."

"That's their trick. They want to make you think it's everywhere, but it's aimed at me and my dog." Morrie owned a nondescript white dust mop of a pooch that he sometimes took downtown on a leash.

"Your best bet is to stay indoors and be as quiet as you can until the snow goes away," I said. "If you keep trying to stop it, the Russians will keep sending more."

"You mean I should just sit in my apartment all day?"

"I mean stay there without talking to anyone until the snow stops. You might even go to bed with a nice glass of wine."

"Oh, I never drink alcohol," Morrie said. "But I will go back to bed."

Thank God he doesn't drink alcohol, I thought as I hung up. I couldn't imagine what phantoms a drunken Morrie would conjure up.

At last I had time to call Brownie. After nine rings, I heard, "Homicidebrown."

"Dailydispatchmitchell," I said. "Anything new on Klondike Kate?"

"As a matter of fact, there is," Brownie said. "The lab has reported a positive match on the fetus's DNA."

"Oh, my god, who?" I yelled loud enough to cause every reporter in the newsroom to look my way.

"The chief will announce that at a 10:00 o'clock media briefing here in the station. Have a good day, Mitch."

"You could have given me a heads-up," I said into the dead phone, making no effort not to sound whiny.

CHAPTER TWENTY-ONE

Who's Your Daddy?

AL AND I ARRIVED AT THE STATION ten minutes early, only to find the room already jammed with TV cameras and reporters bearing microphones. As always, Trish Valentine was right up front.

I wriggled through the mob and pushed in beside her. "Hey, Trish, did you spend the night here or what?" I asked.

"Are you implying that I slept with somebody here?" she replied.

"I didn't say that. I'm just wondering how early you have to get here in order to latch onto the best spot, front and center."

"My cameraman and I took off as soon as we heard about the briefing. I think we've been here about twenty minutes, long enough that my feet are starting to hurt." She was wearing boots with heels high enough to add a couple of inches to her height.

"Those heels must be a pain. Why not wear something more practical?"

"When you're as short as I am, you need a boost. I guess a tall person like you wouldn't understand."

"Well, I'm sure the chief will be happy to see you in the front row anyway."

Trish's reply was cut short when Police Chief Casey O'Malley, Ramsey County Attorney Howard Albert and Homicide Detective Curtis Brown entered the room.

The chief stepped forward and looked sternly over our heads while waiting for the babble to stop.

"We're here this morning to announce that we have determined the identity of the father of the late Lee-Ann Nordquist's unborn baby," O'Malley said when all was quiet. "As you know, we took DNA samples from a several men in this effort. We have been rewarded with a positive match, and we're now searching for the man in question."

The chief paused, which he knew would play well on the TV sound bites, and held the silence until I was ready to scream, "For God's sake, tell us who!"

"The man we are seeking is named Ted Carlson, age thirty-three, who lives in Roseville and works downtown in the Winter Carnival office as liaison for the Vulcans," O'Malley said. Again he paused for effect.

After a collective gasp of amazement from his audience, O'Malley continued, "Mr. Carlson is married, but has been known to be quite friendly with several women connected with the Winter Carnival, including the late Ms. Lee-Ann Nordquist. Mr. Carlson is also known to have been wearing a Vulcan costume on the night of Ms. Nordquist's murder. He also is known to have been in the Crowne Plaza Hotel, again wearing a Vulcan costume, on the night of the attack on Ms. Toni Erickson.

"We attempted to reach Mr. Carlson for questioning this morning, but were told that he left his office immediately upon learning from a reporter that we had received the DNA test results. We have issued an APB on Mr. Carlson, and we ask that you folks inform the public that we are looking for him. We're e-mailing a photo obtained from the Winter Carnival office to all media outlets. Now, are there any questions?"

O'Malley looked expectantly at Trish, and she didn't fail him. "Who was the reporter and why did he warn Carlson?" she asked.

"The reporter will remain unidentified," the chief said. "When this person learned of the new development, he, or she, called Mr. Carlson for a comment, not knowing that he was, shall we say, intimately involved. I wouldn't categorize it as a warning."

After a couple of more questions, the trio called a halt and retreated, leaving the media mob to disperse. Large, wet snowflakes were still falling and sticking to every available surface when Al and I hit the sidewalk.

"Looks like it's up to our ankles so far," I said.

"Think it'll get chest high?" Al asked.

"We'll never bust through if it does," I said.

"T HAT GIRL REALLY GOT AROUND," Jayne Halvorson said as we sat sipping our ginger ale in Herbie's after the Monday night AA meeting. "Screwing one guy regularly and getting pregnant by another one. Anybody you've talked to mention any other boyfriends in the picture?"

I said I hadn't heard of any, but that at least one of this year's Vulcan Krewe had been hoping to get into her bloomers.

"Bet he's damn glad he didn't score right now," Jayne said.

"If he had, she might still be alive," I said. "He was beaten to the draw in O'Halloran's that night by the guy who killed her."

"Such slender threads our lives hang on. How often are we at the mercy of other people's decisions?"

"Too often. Right now Martha is at the mercy of her boss's decision to send her to Duluth. They had a hell of a ride up there through the snow and could have had a serious accident."

"Even a minor accident could be serious in this kind of weather." The snow was still falling and the accumulation reported in the Twin Cities on the 5:00 p.m. news was ten inches. Farther north, the totals were higher, with Duluth reporting fourteen inches, accompanied by winds gusting up to thirty-five miles per hour.

"Martha could be stuck up there for the rest of the winter," I said. "She wasn't even sure they could start jury selection tomorrow because some of the prospective jurors lived out of town, up along the north shore."

Jayne took a swallow of her drink and said, "I take it things are going okay with you two."

"Okay and then some," I said. "Martha even mentioned the word honeymoon last Friday."

"How do you feel about that?"

"Scared. For two reasons. One is the thought of actually taking those vows. The other is that she wants the honeymoon to be on Martha's Vineyard."

"You've got to get over the first reason. I don't know what to say about the second one."

"I can probably talk her out of the Vineyard. The question is can I talk myself into saying the vows."

"I'm betting that you can." She drained the glass and pushed back her chair. "And now I have to go home and make sure my two girls have talked themselves into doing their homework."

I slip-slid through a foot of snow on the sidewalk for three blocks to the serenity of my building, all the while thinking about Martha's out-of-the-blue remark about a honeymoon. I felt like I was teetering at the brink of a precipice, about to topple either into or out of a commitment demanding lifelong fidelity. This seemed even more treacherous than the slippery stuff under my feet.

Sherlock Holmes met me at the door with a meow and a request to have his ears scratched. I knew which way he'd want me to fall. He's always liked Martha best.

TUESDAY WAS MY DAY OFF for the week, and Martha called while I was putting peanut butter on my toast much later than usual. The snow had stopped in both St. Paul and Duluth, but she said the prospect of starting the trial was dim. Several members of the jury pool had called the clerk of court to say the roads were blocked and they couldn't get to the courthouse. If the roads weren't cleared by noon, which was doubtful because the total snowfall around Duluth was twenty-one inches, the start of jury selection would be postponed until Wednesday.

"So what are you going to do up there all day?" I asked.

"Luckily, I packed an extra book," Martha said.

"It better be the size of *War and Peace*. You could be stuck there until after Groundhog Day."

"How much snow would a groundhog hog if a groundhog could hog snow?"

"You'd better give up and catch a plane for home. It sounds like your mind has already gone south."

"Just a variation on the old woodchuck theme. Anyhow, I'll talk to you later, sweetie. Sara's ready to go downstairs for a mid-morning doughnut."

I spent the rest of the morning cleaning up the apartment and running some clothes through the washer and dryer in the basement. Martha called back at about 12:30 with news that jury selection had been postponed until Wednesday morning. I professed a profound lack of astonishment. We talked for half an hour without either of us mentioning the word honeymoon before she had me lift Sherlock to the phone so she could instruct him to continue keeping me warm. We made our usual kissy sounds and hung up.

"What do you think about a honeymoon?" I asked Sherlock Holmes.

He cocked his head slightly, turned around and strolled into the bedroom. Was there feline symbolism in that response?

At 5:00 p.m., I turned on the TV and flipped to Channel 4 in hope of seeing Trish Valentine reporting live about the snowstorm. Sure enough, she was at the airport interviewing some of the hundreds of passengers still waiting for flights delayed by the weather. She looked fetching in form-fitting black ski pants and another form-fitting sweater, this one featuring various shades of red.

Back at the studio, the perpetually-smiling anchorman, Todd Gilmore, announced that St. Paul police had issued a warrant for the arrest of Ted Carlson, who was still missing and considered to be a fugitive from justice. Carlson's picture was shown for fifteen seconds while Gilmore asked residents to watch for him. Police believed Carlson was still in the city because of the difficulty of traveling in the storm. I thought it would be amusing if Trish inadvertently tapped him on the shoulder and asked him for an interview while reporting live from the airport mob scene.

Al called during the next commercial and asked if I'd like to help dispose of a substantial portion of Carol's meatloaf at dinnertime. I jumped on this invitation quicker than a coyote pouncing on a drowsy field mouse. If there was a list of the world's ten worst cooks, I would be near the top, and I had been contemplating a supper consisting of two nuked hotdogs slathered with mustard and wrapped in slices of bread. A chance to feast on Carol's meatloaf was definitely worth plowing through the snow.

After a magnificent meatloaf and mashed potatoes dinner, capped with a slice of hot apple crisp, Al suggested a ritual that we perform at various stages of pursuing a story. This ritual consists of sitting at the computer and culling photos that we were sure wouldn't ever be printed or needed for the files. Because the Klondike Kate murder story was nearing its denouement, pending the arrest and arraignment of Ted Carlson, Al figured he could clear some space on his hard drive by deleting most of the shots pertaining to that story and storing the survivors on a CD.

We started with shots of Lee-Ann Nordquist's body lying in John Robertson Junior's driveway and slowly worked our way toward the Monday press briefing about Carlson's paternity. We were flipping through the dozens of photos Al had shot at the Vulcan Victory Dance when something caught his eye.

"That's different," he said. We were looking at a shot that included a trio of Vulcans toasting their triumph over King Boreas. It had been taken near the end of the evening, a few minutes before Toni Erickson's blood-curdling scream sent everyone scrambling for the ballroom exits.

"What's different?" I asked.

"On the left side, behind those guys. See that Vulcan with his back to us? He's wearing red boots. All the Vulcans I've ever seen wear black boots."

"Oh, shit!" I said. "I know somebody who wears red boots."

CHAPTER TWENTY-TWO

Booting Up

A L FLASHED THROUGH THE ENTIRE COLLECTION of Victory Dance shots again, and we found one more that showed a red-booted Vulcan in the background. It also had been shot only a few minutes before the scream.

"Okay, so your friend Kitty wears red boots," Al said. "But where would she get a Vulcan costume and why would she wear it to the dance?"

"Beats me," I said. "And early in the evening we all saw her—and you photographed her—wearing regular clothes."

"So the red-booted Vulcan probably isn't her."

"Probably not. But we need to find out for sure."

"So, how do you plan to do that?" Al asked. "Call her up and say, 'Hey, Kitty baby, did you wear a Vulcan costume and your sexy red boots to the Victory Dance?'"

"It'll take somewhat more finesse than that," I said.

"Do you have a plan based on this finesse? Or even a plan based on your usual lack of finesse?"

"Not off the top of my head, but I'll think of something. If we can eliminate Kitty as the Vulcan in red boots, we can go to work on finding out which member of which Krewe has red boots."

"What if this is Kitty in the picture?"

"Then we find out why she's wearing this get-up. And I think I'm getting an idea of how to do it."

"So enlighten me as to how you'll quiz Miss Kitty."

"Well, the best way to catch a kitty is to entice it with food and petting, right?" I said. "This Kitty has been coming on to me since the day we met, but I cooled her off the last time by saying

I was working on a commitment with Martha. Suppose I call Kitty and use that commitment thing—tell her that Martha has dumped me—and ask her to have dinner with me? And suppose I invite her to my apartment after dinner? As you know, Martha is away until God knows when. Then, when the moment gets mellow, I show Kitty a print of your photo and ask if it's her."

"And what if she says yes, it is her?"

"Then you'll pop out of the closet, where you've been hiding, and record the moment with your trusty camera."

"Are you going to get the lady naked before you pop the question?" Al asked.

"As close as possible," I said. "I figure the less clothing she's wearing the less likely she'll be to run out into the cold when I show her the picture."

"In that case, how about I drill a peephole in your closet door?"

"I'm shocked that you'd even think of resorting to voyeurism," I said.

"I'm just thinking that you might need an eye witness," he said. "Think of it as your witness protection program."

"Keeping you in the dark is the best witness protection program I can think of."

I WAS ITCHING LIKE A MONKEY with its armpits full of fleas to call Kitty Catalano the minute her office opened at 9:00 a.m. on Wednesday, but timing was important. I was afraid that if I jumped on the phone first thing, I'd sound impetuous. I wanted her to think I'd been brooding, so I controlled the urge to call for almost an hour. My goal was to come across as wounded and down in the mouth, not salivating over prospects for an after-dinner roll in the hay. If I could convince her that I needed solace, I was sure that she'd suggest a suitable method.

I filled part of the waiting time with a call to Detective Curtis Brown. He informed me that Ted Carlson had not been apprehended, but that every possible means of departure was under observation.

"You can't have every road blocked," I said.

"His wife told us where he parks his car when he's downtown, and we found it there," Brownie said. "He's either going to bail out by air, train, or bus. We've got all those stations covered."

"You're sure he didn't beat you to the draw? He could have been long gone before you set up surveillance."

"That's true, but nothing has showed up on any of his credit cards. No tickets for transportation of any kind, no motels."

"Maybe he's a cash customer," I said.

"Whatever. Have a good day, Mitch."

When I finally called Kitty, I got her voice mail. She was either out or on another call. "Please, God, don't let her be out for long," I whispered after I left a message and put down the phone.

She wasn't. The return call came exactly sixteen minutes later. Not that I was watching the clock.

"Hi, Mitch," Kitty said. "What can I do for you?"

"You can give my shattered ego and sagging morale a boost," I said in a flat, expressionless voice.

"Wow, that's quite an order. What's going on?"

"It's what's not going on. You know that commitment project I told I've been working on? It's been de-committed, so to speak."

"The woman left you?"

"She took off for Duluth with somebody else," I said. I didn't even have to lie.

"That sucks," Kitty said. "You want to have dinner or something?"

"Maybe dinner and something," I said.

"Ooh, that sounds like fun. Where do you want to eat? Before the something, that is."

I really liked the way this conversation was going. I suggested a restaurant and Kitty said that would be great. "I've got some errands to run after work, but I could meet you at the restaurant at seven," she added.

"Sounds great," I said. "I feel better already."

"Glad to hear it. See you soon."

"Oh, hey!" I said, catching her before she hung up. "Wear your red boots. They're really a turn-on."

"Anything you say, Mr. Shattered Ego."

I put down the phone and walked quick-time to the photo department where Al was working on his late-morning coffee and doughnut.

"She bit," I said. "Took it hook, line, and sinker."

"Great," Al said. "When do we reel her in?"

We estimated that dinner would take about an hour and a half, which meant that Kitty and I would be starting for my place to do our "something" at about 8:30. Al would use the key I keep hidden in a shrub near the parking lot door to get into my apartment. I would go to the men's room before leaving the restaurant and call his cell phone so he could tuck himself away in the bedroom closet.

The layout of my apartment is simple. From the hall, you enter through the kitchen/dining area and turn left to go into the living room. From there it's a straight shot to the bedroom, where the bathroom is on the right and the closet, with sliding doors, faces the foot of the bed. My plan was to get Kitty into the bedroom and at least partially undressed before showing her the picture. My thought was that the lack of clothing would prevent a sudden departure, and the element of surprise would bring forth an honest answer if she was, in fact, the Vulcan in red boots.

At noon, Martha called to say that jury selection had been postponed again because at least a dozen people in the pool were still stranded on unplowed roads. The judge vowed to begin the process on Thursday morning, no matter how many prospects were missing, but it looked like Martha's sojourn in Duluth would carry over into the following week.

"Bummer," I said. "I want you home tomorrow." I refrained from adding, "But not tonight."

"Me, too," Martha said. "I miss sleeping with Sherlock Holmes."

The afternoon dragged by, the way time does when you're eager for it to fly. When the clock finally got around to 5:00 p.m., I shut down my computer, put on my coat and went home. I took a shower and changed into a fresh powder-blue shirt and black pants. I topped this combination off with a red tie and my best navy blazer. Just before leaving the apartment, I tucked a tiny tape recorder loaded with a thirty-minute tape into my shirt pocket. I arrived at the restaurant at 6:58 and was led to the table that I'd reserved. Five minutes later, when Kitty was escorted to the table and took off her coat, every head in the restaurant turned in her direction.

She was wearing the red boots all right. And above them she was dressed in full Klondike Kate regalia, a low-cut red blouse with puffy short sleeves and a red skirt with black trim over a full white petticoat. Her long, dark-brown hair was flowing free and her green eyes were sparkling. The effect was as spectacular as it was surprising.

I rose from my chair, and she wrapped her arms around me and kissed me on the mouth, letting her lips linger longer than necessary for a friendly hello. When we parted, the other diners were all studying their plates or staring at their table settings. Being Minnesotans, they were embarrassed by Kitty's un-Minnesota-like public display of affection and they couldn't bear to look at us.

"My ego is rising already," I said when we were seated. Her signature perfume, which teased my nostrils during the kiss, had permeated my mustache and was lingering there.

"My mission is to raise your ego and anything else that needs raising," Kitty said.

"I'm sure you'll be able to accomplish your mission. You can look forward to my complete cooperation."

This witty repartee was interrupted by our server, a round, rosy-cheeked young man named Taylor, who took our drink orders—wine for Kitty and coffee for me—and hustled away.

"I asked for the red boots, but I wasn't expecting a full Kate costume," I said.

"I wear this when I introduce the Kates at special occasions," Kitty said. "And I figured this was a special occasion."

"I'm flattered, and flattery will get you everywhere."

"Everywhere is a good destination. I'd say I'm sorry that your friend ran off to Duluth, but I'd be lying. I think most media people are assholes, but you're different somehow."

"Must be my boyish charm," I said. "But beware. I can be as big an asshole as the next guy."

"I doubt it. You're just not the asshole type."

"Again I'm flattered."

She responded by reaching under the table and caressing my leg a couple of inches above the kneecap. I reached under and laid my hand on the back of hers. I don't know where our hands would have wandered next if Taylor hadn't returned right then with the wine and coffee.

To say dinner passed pleasantly would be an understatement. We talked and laughed about a wide range of topics without ever mentioning the killing of one Klondike Kate or the attack on another. In fact, I'd had so much fun with Kitty I was feeling guilt pangs as I walked back to the restroom to make my cell phone call to Al. Here was this bright, gorgeous, fun-loving woman eager to share the night with me, and here was I, setting her up for a sneak attack. However, I made the call, and Al said he'd be in the closet when we arrived.

"My place?" I said, as I helped Kitty slide into her coat.

"I have a better idea," Kitty said. "The Winter Carnival keeps a Jacuzzi suite in the Crowne Plaza for VIPs when they come to town. It's vacant tonight and I have a key. We could do the hot bath bit together before getting all wrapped up doing that something you were talking about this morning."

Here was an unexpected glitch. "That sounds great, but I've got my place all ready with candlelight and champagne for the lady." I had, in fact, put a small bottle of bubbly into the fridge.

"We can order champagne in the hotel," she said. "The room is gorgeous and the Jacuzzi is marvelous. I love to get naked and soak in hot, swirling water with a guy before I, uh, do something with him." We had stopped just inside the front door of the restaurant and she breathed the last sentence into my right ear, which caused a rise in my overall body temperature.

Still, I resisted. "But you can't justify taking me there," I said. "I'm not a VIP."

"Nobody needs to know except the maid who makes up the room," Kitty said. "And she'll be quiet if she receives a small token of gratitude from me. This will be way better for your poor, limp ego than going to your apartment, which must have some sad memories now that your lover has left you."

I couldn't see a way out of this. If I kept insisting on my apartment, she'd probably think I was planning some sort of perversion and had set up a complex of chains and whips. I'd have to yield to her invitation, and find a moment to call Al and inform him of the change in venue. "Okay, the Jacuzzi suite it is," I said. "Shall we both take our cars and meet there?"

"Let's go in my car," Kitty said. "I can drive you back to yours in the morning."

"We'll have to get up awfully early. Tomorrow's a work day. Maybe we'd better take both cars."

"I don't mind getting up early if you don't. Maybe we can have another little something if we wake up early enough."

How does a guy counter that without looking like a dork? I agreed to ride in her car, which turned out to be a black BMW, and gave up on my plan to call Al from my car on the way to the hotel.

As Kitty parked the Beemer facing a wall in the ramp attached to the hotel, I noticed that no light was reflecting off the concrete on the passenger side. "Looks like you've got a headlight out on this side," I said.

"It's been out for a couple of weeks," Kitty said. "I keep forgetting to get it fixed. It's no big deal"

"You should get it done. You're lucky you haven't been stopped by the cops. One time in Wisconsin, I was stopped less than ten minutes after a light went out."

"Some of us just live right," she said.

On the elevator, Kitty pressed the button for the twenty-first floor.

"I'm impressed," I said as the elevator began to rise. "The very top floor."

"Nothing but the best for the Winter Carnival," Kitty said.

I followed her down the hall to room 2112, where she slid her plastic key into the slot and the green light flashed. She opened the door, stepped in, turned on the light, seized my hand and drew me in. "Entree, Monsieur Mitchell," she said, emphasizing the second syllable of my name.

She was right. The room was gorgeous, not to mention huge. Two of the walls were made up of rows of windows adorned with drapes. One row of windows overlooked the Mississippi River, which must have been spectacular in daylight. The Jacuzzi sat in the far corner where the windowed walls joined, opposite the bathroom and kitty-corner from a bed that would have filled my bedroom wall to wall. This room had yards of open space, even though it also contained a sofa, an armchair, several potted plants and a bar.

"Isn't this just a wee bit better than your apartment?" Kitty asked.

"About the same," I said. "The only things my bedroom doesn't have are the windows, the Jacuzzi, the football-field-size bed and the several hundred square feet of floor space."

"I knew you'd love it when you saw it. Shall I order champagne for two?"

"Only for one. You really don't want to see me turn into a slobbering, staggering mass of mush."

"Then I'll skip it, too. Why don't we get started with the Jacuzzi?"

"Good idea," I said. "Why don't you turn it on while I take a quick pit stop? All that coffee is hitting bottom."

Kitty kissed me again on the lips, putting some tongue into the action this time, and breathed the word "okay" into that lucky right ear. She headed for the Jacuzzi while I went into the bathroom and closed the door. I pulled out my cell phone and punched in Al's number. After six rings I got his voice mail. I should have realized that he'd turn off his phone when he went into the closet so it wouldn't ring at an inopportune moment.

"Damn it," I said before the beep. "There's been a change," I said after the beep, hoping that he'd turn on his phone when we didn't show up after a reasonable amount of time. "Crowne Plaza room 2112. Get your ass over here to back me up."

I took off my blazer, loosened my tie, switched on my pocket tape recorder and walked out of the bathroom with the blazer over my arm. Again I said, "Wow!"

CHAPTER TWENTY-THREE

Action and Distraction

ITTY STOOD FACING ME WEARING ONLY a white push-up bra, bright red knee-length bloomers and the red boots. Her blouse, skirt and petticoat were piled in a scarlet and white heap on the floor near the Jacuzzi, which was filling with water.

"You like?" she asked, thrusting a rounded hip in my direction.

"How could I not?" I said. "You're absolutely gorgeous."

"There's lots more to see." Kitty bent over, tugged at the elastic waist of her bloomers, slid them down her long legs until they covered the tops of her boots and straightened up. My eyes must have popped six inches out of my head because she laughed out loud at my expression.

Looking up at me from the curve of her lower belly and crotch was the face of a brown-and-black striped cat—ears, eyes, nose, whiskers, and a mouth that would open vertically. I had seen this kind of crazy body painting on the Internet because a friend had e-mailed a site with two dozen pictures showing both sexes naked and decorated, but I never imagined that I would come face to female flesh with it. If the word "discombobulated" was illustrated in the dictionary, my photo would have been there at that moment.

"Like my pretty pussy?" Kitty asked. "If you pet her, I bet she'll purr."

I realized my mouth was hanging open, so I closed it. Then I tried to form words with it and failed. Finally, I mumbled, "Izza tattoo?"

Kitty cocked her head, indicating that my meaning had not been perfectly clear.

I swallowed, took a deep breath and tried to gather my wits before speaking again. On my second try, I managed to enunciate. "Is that a tattoo?"

She laughed again. "No, silly, it's only paint. You can't put a tattoo on pubic hair. I have a friend who does this kind of artwork on people, but not usually on this particular part of a person. It'll wash off in about a week. I got it special for you to cheer you up. That was the errand I had to run after work."

"I envy the artist," I said. "I wish I could paint on a canvas like that."

Still laughing, Kitty took a step toward me, but staggered and almost fell because her movement was constricted by the bloomers wrapped around the tops of her boots.

Her boots. Damn it, that's what I was there for. In the literal heat of the moment, I'd forgotten that my reason for meeting this woman was business and not erotic entertainment. I was supposed to quiz her about the goddamn boots, not, as she suggested, make her hand-painted pussycat purr.

I took a deep breath and said, "I've got something to show you, too."

"That's pretty obvious," she said, waving a hand toward the tell-tale bulge in my trousers. "Why don't we get rid of all our clothes and get in the Jacuzzi and pretend we're a couple of honeymooners?"

Honeymooners? Oh, my god, no! Not here. Not a Jacuzzi honeymoon with Kitty. If there was a honeymoon, it had to be on an island with Martha. "I don't mean this," I said, looking where she was pointing. "I need to show you a picture."

I reached into the inside pocket of the blazer still draped over my arm, pulled out the photo and handed it to her. Al had cropped and enlarged the image so that the red-booted Vulcan was the focal point.

The laughter stopped and Kitty's eyes turned to green chips of flint. "Where did you get this?" she asked.

"My buddy Al shot this at the Vulcan Victory Dance," I said. "We wondered if those were your red boots. Are they?"

"What if they are?"

"If they are, I assume that it's you in the Vulcan costume. Why would you be wearing that?"

"You nosy son of a bitch," she said. "You were right. You can be as big an asshole as all the other reporters."

Kitty bent down and the provocative pussycat disappeared as she pulled her bloomers back up around her waist. Then she stooped again, reached into her right boot and brought out something shiny. It was a miniature snub-nose pistol just like the one Sean Fitzpatrick had carried into our office to show us how easily it could be hidden.

"These boots are good for more than walking," she said. "They're just roomy enough to carry this little piece of security."

It was amazing how much bigger that size gun looked in Kitty's hand than it had in Fitzpatrick's mitt. The muzzle, which was pointing at my chest, looked big enough to fire a cannon ball, and I took an involuntary step backward. A quick glance over my shoulder told me I was too far from the bathroom door to make a dash and lock myself in.

Kitty saw the move and read my mind. "Don't even think about running for the john," she said. "From this range I could put a bullet right between your shoulder blades before you got to the door."

"Would you like to tell me what this is all about?" I wondered if Al had grown tired of waiting yet and had switched on his cell phone to discover a missed call.

"Why not? It looks like I'm going to have to shoot you because you tried to rape me, so I might as well tell you all about it."

"My guess is that you put on the suit that night to kill Toni Erickson, and that you wore it the previous week when you killed Lee-Ann Nordquist. Am I right?"

"Give yourself an 'A,' Mr. Asshole Reporter."

"What I can't guess is how you got the suit and why you wanted to kill those women," I said.

"Let me start with Lee-Ann, may she rot in hell," Kitty said. "I've hated her guts for two years, and I saw the perfect chance to get rid of the whoring little bitch."

"Everybody seemed to love Lee-Ann. Why'd you hate her so much?" The longer I could drag this out, the better chance I had of hearing Al knock on the door. I hoped that the sound of his knock would distract Kitty long enough for me to make a grab for the gun.

"Two reasons," she said. "Number one: remember I told you that when I followed my boyfriend here from Madison I found out that he was banging somebody else? Well, guess who it was."

"Lee-Ann?"

"Give yourself another 'A.' Charlie said he'd discovered that he preferred full-figured women. In other words, he liked big tits and a chubby ass. He got what he had coming two months later when she dumped him and moved on to her next lover boy."

"Okay, I understand that one. What was your second reason to hate her?"

"The bitch beat me out for Klondike Kate, just because of those big tits and chubby ass. I won the talent show hands down. Lee-Ann had a voice like a chain saw when she sang, but she got the title because I was too skinny."

"Did you take the office job so you'd have a chance to kill her?" I asked.

"I took the job so I could be around her and mess up her life some way," Kitty said. "I didn't plan to kill her until that night, when I saw her drinking in O'Halloran's with a bunch of Vulcans. I thought how easy it would be to knock her off and have the cops go hunting for one of them.

"I knew the Vulcans' room would be empty, so I ran back here and got a key from the desk on the pretense that one of my Vulcan friends had left his wallet up there. There were three or four costumes laid out on chairs, and I picked one that fit pretty well. In fact, it probably was the one you wore when you went around with the Vulcans on Friday."

I couldn't keep still. "You killed her in the suit that I wore?" That's why Kitty's perfume had seemed familiar. I'd smelled a trace of it in the running suit.

"Like I said, it probably was," Kitty said. "It was a little long, but with the bottom tucked into my boots, who cared? Anyway, I put on the suit and found some grease paint so I could smear on a beard. My only problem was that there weren't any boots. They'd all taken their boots home to polish. I was wearing my red ones, so I said the hell with it and put them back on. Then I dropped my clothes off at my car, went back to O'Halloran's and offered to buy the bitch a drink."

"How'd you fool Lee-Ann?" I asked. "Didn't your voice give you away?"

Kitty's response came in a voice an octave lower than normal. "I told you I majored in theater. One of my talents is doing impressions. I do men as well as women. Want to hear me do Darth Vader?"

"You can't do Darth Vader."

The voice dropped another half-octave. "Beware, young Skywalker, I'm about to blast off your dick with my light sword."

I clapped my hands three times and took a step toward her. Kitty backed off a step and warned me not to come any closer if I wanted to hear the rest of her story before she pulled the trigger. I smiled, shrugged and abandoned my plan to creep close enough to tackle the gun. I'd have to wait for Al's knock on the door.

"Okay, tell me. How did you kill Lee-Ann?" I asked.

"I got her shit-faced on vodka tonics, which only took a couple because she was already half in the bag, and offered to drive her to my place for some sex," Kitty said. "She'd fuck anything in pants, so she accepted the invitation. I went with her to get her coat, which was hanging way in the back, by the restrooms. When she reached for the coat, I whipped the cord around her neck from behind and yanked it so tight she couldn't even gurgle."

"So she was already dead when you were seen helping her out the door like such a gentleman?"

"You bet your ass she was."

"Why didn't you wait to kill her until you had her back in your apartment?"

"If I did that, I'd have a body in my apartment to dispose of. This way, I could just dump her somewhere and go home."

"Why'd you drive way out to Mississippi River Boulevard?" I asked.

"I was looking for a place that was quiet and dark, and I found it out there," she said. "The people in those houses were all in bed and there's not much traffic at that time of night. I had time to lay her out and even bruise her crotch to make it look like attempted rape. After that, I went back to the hotel with my clothes, changed back and returned the Vulcan suit. Laid it all out nice for somebody to pick up and put on."

"And that somebody was me," I said. I felt my dinner rising a bit at the thought of that, but I swallowed hard and kept the conversation going. "You said something about Lee-Ann, uh, screwing anything in pants. Were you stretching it a bit because of what she did with your boyfriend?"

"No way. I heard the bitch tell one of her buddies that she laid most of the guys on last year's Vulcan Krewe."

"I interviewed all the married ones. They all said they barely knew her."

"Barely knew her? Bullshit! Those bastards knew her . . . what's the term? Intimately, I think it is. Some of them, anyway. And I'm not surprised that it's Ted Carlson that knocked her up. He's always sniffing around the Kates. Tried to take me out for drinks more than once."

"You don't like Ted?"

"I don't like messing around with married men. Big waste of time if you ask me."

"You put on a great act after you killed Lee-Ann. Hitting high 'C' when I called you and carrying on all teary-eyed about how bad you felt to lose a sister Kate. Standing up at the funeral and announcing the scholarship was really a cute touch. Your college theater director would be proud of your performance."

"Thank you. It's too bad you won't be around to write a review."

"Okay, so now I understand why you killed Lee-Ann," I said. "But why did you try to kill Toni?"

"Because the idiot was going around the dance telling everybody she knew who killed Lee-Ann," Kitty said.

"Are you the caller with the deep voice who threatened her?"

"You got it. Anyhow I thought maybe she really had figured it out, so that night I ran up to the Vulcans' dressing room, changed into the Vulcan suit and came back to the dance."

"Were you planning to get her drunk, too?"

"Didn't need to. Toni has a bladder problem and can't go more than an hour without peeing. I just slipped into the ladies' when nobody was around, hid in a stall and waited for her to come in."

"Toni said she slugged her attacker in the crotch, but it didn't seem to hurt. Now I understand why it didn't work the way it should have."

"Give yourself a third 'A.' That punch hurt, but it didn't do the kind of damage it does to somebody with balls."

"But still you got caught in the act."

"I thought that other woman had gone out. Somebody else must have banged the door twice."

"Speaking of bangs, do you always carry that gun?" I asked, wondering how much longer I could stall. Where in the hell was Al? He couldn't still be waiting in the goddamn closet.

"Only when I think I might need it," Kitty said. "When you called and gave me your sob story, I got a little suspicious because you're a reporter and because you seemed pretty loyal to your girlfriend when I was coming on to you just a couple of days ago. So I took little Ms. Derringer along as insurance and I'm damn glad I did. But I've gotta say you were good. You had me thinking that you really wanted to take me to bed until you pulled out that picture."

"I really did want to take you to bed. Unfortunately, my first priority was checking out those red boots."

"I bet your woman didn't really go to Duluth, did she?"

"Actually, she did. But she went with another woman lawyer because they're working at a trial."

"That's why you were able to invite me to your place tonight."

"Voila," I said.

"Well, if it's any comfort to you, this suite is a lot classier place to die. Which is what's going to happen to you right now."

"You won't get away with it," I said. Immediately I felt embarrassment at spouting such a stale cliché.

"Why not?" Kitty said. "I've got the perfect story to tell the cops. We had dinner, we talked about the Winter Carnival, I brought you up here just to show you the room because you said you'd like to see it, and you got all excited and turned on the Jacuzzi while I was in the bathroom. When I came out, you were standing there naked, and you came at me and tried to rip off my clothes. We tussled, and you were so strong that I was forced to shoot you in self-defense. It's lucky I had the gun or I'd have been raped and maybe killed. Now take off your shoes and socks, and don't even think about throwing one of them at me."

She took another step back, increasing the shoe-tossing range. I pulled off my shoes and socks, being careful not to bend over so far that the tape recorder would fall out of my shirt pocket, and asked what to do next.

"Take off your pants," she said. "Too bad you lost what I wanted to look at." Indeed, my sexual arousal had dropped away. I took off my pants, again being careful not to bend too far forward.

"Have you got a back problem or what?" Kitty asked. "You move like you've got a rod up your ass."

"I do have a problem with a couple of disks," I said. "It's very painful for me to bend over very far."

"Well, it won't be hurting you any more. Get over by the Jacuzzi and take off your shorts." We did a circle dance, with me moving to the Jacuzzi and her sliding toward the door.

I was standing with my back to the Jacuzzi and starting to pull down my under shorts when the doorknob rattled. Kitty turned her head toward the sound in time to see the door open. I yanked up my shorts and started running toward her, yelling, "Al, get away from the door!"

Chapter Twenty-Four

A Bang-up Exit

IT WASN'T AL STANDING IN THE DOORWAY. It was Ted Carlson. Immediately behind him was a woman I recognized as Angela Rinaldi, even though she was not dressed in her Klondike Kate costume.

Kitty spun sideways, keeping the gun pointed at me, and said, "Stop right there." I stopped.

"What the hell are you doing here?" Carlson yelled.

Kitty swung the gun toward him. "Get out of my way, Ted."

"What the hell are you doing?" he yelled again.

"I'm leaving," Kitty said. She turned and ran toward the door, and I started chasing her again. I almost had my hand on her shoulder when the gun went off with a bang not much louder than a firecracker.

Carlson screamed and fell backward against Angela, and they both crashed to the floor. Angela landed on her butt with Carlson sprawled on top of her. Kitty jumped over their thrashing legs like a Green Bay running back heading for the Vikings' goal line and went racing down the hall toward the stairway.

I hesitated for a moment in shock before I followed, leaping over the floundering couple on the floor and running down the hall about thirty feet behind Kitty. I yelled at her to stop, and suddenly she did. So did I because she turned and pointed the little pistol my way. I hit the deck on my belly, buried my nose in the carpet and got my nostrils filled with dust as she fired.

The slug ricocheted off the rug in front of me and burned a skin-deep furrow across the tip of my right shoulder, ruining my shirt and causing a small river—a creek, actually—of blood to begin dribbling down my arm. I raised my head in time to see Kitty disappear through the stairway door.

She had twenty flights of stairs to run down, plus a seventy-five-yard dash to her car, clad only her bra, bloomers and boots. I thought that if I called the front desk, hotel security would be able to head her off. I pushed myself up to a standing position and almost went back down because my knees were shaking so violently. I had to prop myself up against the wall and take a series of deep breaths before my legs were steady enough to carry me back to room 2112, where I could use the phone to call the desk.

When I got there, I found Carlson lying on his back with a red stain spreading across the middle of his white shirt. Angela was kneeling beside him with tears streaming down her cheeks and high notes screeching from her mouth.

I grabbed Angela by the shoulders. "Shut up while I call 911," I said. She looked at me like I was from another galaxy and let out another scream. I shook her, told her again to shut up and went into the room to grab the phone. I heard Carlson moan in pain as I was pressing zero.

When the desk clerk answered, I told him to call 911 because a man had been shot on the twenty-first floor. "After that, get hotel security into the garage to stop a woman wearing red boots, bloomers, and a bra," I said. "But tell them to be careful because she's also got a gun."

"Sir, are you serious?" the clerk asked.

"I'm not playing games and I'm not drunk. Do both of those things as fast as you can."

Angela had stopped screaming when I rejoined her at Carlson's side. As I knelt there, I heard another voice ask, "What the hell is going on?"

I looked up to see Al standing over us. "It's about time you got here," I said.

"That man's bleeding and so are you," Al said.

"Your powers of observation never cease to amaze me," I said. "We've both been shot by the red-boot girl."

Carlson's eyes were closed, and he moaned again as I gingerly tugged his shirttails out of his pants, unbuttoned the shirt, spread it open and pulled up his undershirt. Blood was seeping from a hole in the fleshy part of his left side below the rib cage. Apparently the slug hadn't hit an artery or anything vital.

I asked Angela if she had a hanky. She fished around in her purse and pulled out a lacy white one. I pressed the cloth against the wound and saw of a series of flashes from above as Al shot photos of the action. I told Angela to hold the hanky in place, and backed off so Al could get some shots that didn't include me.

When I stood up, the sensation of liquid trickling down my arm and a sharp stinging in my shoulder reminded me that Carlson wasn't the only person who'd been shot. I started to reach for my shoulder with my left hand, but stopped when I saw the fingers were stained with Carlson's blood.

Al saw my problem. "I'll hold the fort here while you go wash your hands and put a towel or something over your shoulder to soak up the blood," he said. "It might also be smart to put on some pants before the cops get here."

I'd forgotten that I was trotting around in my under shorts. "Right," I said. "One should never greet police officers in one's casual under attire."

"You must have been having a pretty good time before the shooting broke out."

"You'll never believe part of it, but the fun was coming to an end. Carlson took a bullet originally intended for me."

I left Al to ponder that while I washed my hands thoroughly, draped a towel over my shoulder and clamped it between my arm and my rib cage so I could slip into my pants. I was zipping up the fly when three uniformed hotel security men skidded to a halt beside Al. I buckled my belt and went out to meet them.

"Did your guys catch the woman in the garage?" I asked.

"What woman's that?" asked a stocky, red-faced man wearing a name tag that said JOHN.

"I told the desk clerk to send security to the garage to head off the woman who shot this guy," I said.

"Clerk never said nothin' about no woman," John said. "Sent us up here to see about a shootin'." The other two men shook their heads.

"Shit, that means Kitty got away," I said. "Did the idiot who sent you up here bother to call 911?"

"Don't know," said John. "Be a good idea if he did."

My question was answered almost immediately when one of the elevators opened and three EMTs and two uniformed cops came dashing down the hall. They'd barely reached us when the other elevator opened and two plainclothes officers stepped out. The one in the lead was Detective Mike Reilly.

"Jesus, Mary, and Joseph," Reilly said when he saw Al and me. "You two again? Why is it every time I go to a crime scene, you two are there?"

"Just lucky, I guess," Al said.

"For you maybe," Reilly said. "Not for me."

"Not for me, either," I said. "I'm one of the wounded." I pointed with my left hand to the towel wrapped around my opposite shoulder.

"Oh, Christ," Reilly said. "Now you're a victim as well as a witness?"

"It pains me to say that that's true," I said.

"I'll testify to that," Al said.

"Just get out of the way for a minute while I talk to the EMTs," Reilly said.

Angela rose from the floor and held up her bloody hands as the EMTs took over on Carlson. She was staring at her palms like Lady Macbeth in the sleepwalking scene, and her face was the color of Uncle Ben's rice.

"Come with me," I said. I took Angela by the arm and steered her to the bathroom. After another splash of Ted Carlson's blood went down the drain, she emerged looking more alive.

"What were you doing here with Ted?" I asked in a whisper.

"We were going to spend the night here," Angela said. "He's been hiding at my place and we were afraid the cops might come there. We were going to hide here and I was going to sneak him out of town in the back of my SUV tomorrow."

"You've been hiding Ted from the cops? Why?"

"I know he didn't kill Lee-Ann, and I love him. He's going to leave his wife and marry me."

"I'll bet he is."

She started to cry. "He is, damn it. If he lives from getting shot."

"He'll live," I said. "It's a flesh wound. He's got a much better chance of getting well than you have of getting married to him."

"What do you know about it?" Angela said. "He said he loves me more than anything in the world."

"You and about a dozen others, so I've heard tell. But maybe you'll be the lucky one. At least you're right about him not killing Lee-Ann."

Our discussion was interrupted by Reilly, who said he had some questions for both of us, starting with Angela. She was beginning to wobble a bit, so I suggested he let her sit down. Reilly scowled at me and waved her toward the armchair. He was standing in front of her, asking questions, when Al walked up beside me and suggested turning off the Jacuzzi. I caught it with the water barely an inch from the top.

"That was close," Al said as I sat on the edge of the Jacuzzi and pulled on my socks and shoes. "And speaking of close, Martha was coming into your apartment as I was going out."

"What the hell was she doing home?" I asked.

"She said something about the case getting settled during the delay and she asked me where you were."

"Oh, God, what did you tell her?"

"I said you were working and that I didn't have time to chat, see you later. You're going to have some major explaining to do. You'll need to be very creative."

"I would be very creative, except it's all going to be in the paper," I said. "Most of it, anyway. I can leave out some of the gory details, but when Martha hears that the cops are looking for a woman wearing nothing but a bra and bloomers and boots, I could be in major doo-doo."

While waiting for Reilly to question me, I got on the cell phone to the *Daily Dispatch* city desk. It was after 10:00 p.m., and Fred Donlin, the night city editor, was in charge. I told him to save some space on page one for Al and me because we were at the scene of a shooting.

"We heard it on the police radio and I was just going to send some people over there," Fred said. "How soon can you and Al get here?"

"I'm not sure," I said. "I'm one of the guys who got shot and dear Detective Reilly wants to question me. Al can get away right now with his pix." Al heard this, waved goodbye and left.

"You got shot?" Fred said. "Why aren't you in the hospital?"

"It just took off some skin. There's an EMT checking me out right now." This was almost true. One of the EMTs was headed my way with her kit in hand. I said goodbye to Fred and gritted my teeth while the EMT, who said her name was Georgia, cut the sleeve off my shirt, cleaned the wound, coated it with liquid fire and taped on a layer of gauze.

"This is just a temporary patch," Georgia said. "You need to go to the hospital as soon as the detective is done with you."

"Right," I said. "Thanks for the patch." There'd be a long stop at the *Daily Dispatch* and a heavy frost in Hades before I took a trip to the hospital.

Reilly asked me some routine questions and shook his head in disbelief when I told him that Kitty Catalano had admitted killing Lee-Ann Nordquist. "No way," he said. "It was a guy in a Vulcan suit."

"I've got her confession on tape," I said, pulling the mini-recorder out of my shirt pocket. The thirty-minute tape had run out, but I was sure it had been going all the while Kitty was telling her story.

"Bring that with you and report to Detective Brown first thing in the morning," Reilly said. "I'm going to leave him a memo so he'll be expecting you, and your ass will be grass if you don't show up." He pushed me out of the room, strung a strip of yellow plastic tape across the door and walked away, followed by the rest of the police brigade. Carlson had been loaded onto a gurney and rolled to the elevator, with Angela tagging along for the ambulance ride.

I opted not to put on my blazer before making the two-block walk to the office, but I did have to get into my top coat because it was fifteen degrees outside. The movement and the contact reignited the fire in my shoulder, but I considered myself lucky that the slug hadn't struck any bones. When I got to my desk at the *Daily Dispatch*, I was encircled by the entire night staff, all of them asking questions but none offering sympathy to the wounded warrior.

"I'll talk to you guys later," I said while I carefully slid the coat off my wounded shoulder. "Now I need to write. Scat!"

They scatted, and I wrote cautiously, leaving out such mundane minutiae as Kitty displaying the artwork on her crotch and my being forced to remove my pants. By the time I had finished and forwarded the story to Fred, the newsroom was almost empty. While Fred was reading the story, Al came to my desk and said he was heading for home. Fred asked me a couple of questions, said it was a fabulous story, sent it to composing and bade me goodnight.

I shut down my computer, struggled into my coat again, picked up my blazer and started toward the door, ready for the drive home. Then reality hit me. My car was still in the restaurant parking lot, two miles away.

CHAPTER TWENTY-FIVE

Playing Pickup

LOOKING AROUND THE NEWSROOM, I saw that the only other people in residence were an assistant editor and a reporter who were standing watch through the night in case of a fire, major accident or freakish storm. I couldn't ask either of them for a ride home.

A bus was out of the question. It was a few minutes before midnight and I had no idea what the late night/early morning transit schedule might be.

My options were to call a taxi or call Martha. I walked back to my desk, took a deep breath and punched in the number for the phone beside our bed.

"I need a pick-me-up," I said when Martha answered.

"Where the hell are you?" Martha said just below a scream. "Al said you were at work, but when I called there you didn't answer your phone, and the desk said they hadn't seen you or heard from you."

"You called too early. I've been in the office for a little over an hour. My problem is that my car isn't here. Could you please come and get me?"

"What happened to your car?" The decibel level and tone were still far above normal. "Did you have an accident?"

"The car is fine. No accident. It's just parked a long way away and it's too long a story to tell on the phone. Please just come and get me and I'll tell you all about it."

"Okay," Martha said in a calmer voice. "I'll have to get dressed, so it'll be a few minutes."

"I'll be watching for you from inside the front door," I said.

Nine minutes later, Martha's Toyota rolled to a stop in front of the *Daily Dispatch* and I scurried out of the lobby and slid into the passenger seat. Martha leaned over and kissed me on the lips before stepping on the gas pedal.

"That was quick," I said. "I wasn't expecting you for another five minutes or so."

"I didn't bother with underwear," she said. "Just threw on my running suit and a jacket."

This was good news. When we got home, she could take off her minimal garments as quickly as she'd put them on. But, just as I was fantasizing her slipping out of the running pants, the pressure from the car's shoulder harness reminded me that maybe this wouldn't be a good night for reckless passion.

Martha was sniffing. "You smell like perfume. You've been with a woman."

"Oh, God, have I ever," I said. "Just take me home, feed me some chicken soup and I'll tell you the whole story before you read it in the paper." Well, almost the whole story.

She nodded. "You're carrying your sport coat. Why aren't you wearing it?"

"That's part of the story. I got nicked a tiny bit by a bullet."

"A bullet!" she yelled. "Why the hell aren't you in the hospital?"

"It's just a little-bitty flesh wound and the EMT took care of it. Let's go get that chicken soup."

In the dark interior of the car, I could sense, rather than see, that she was frowning. "Sorry," she said. "Hospital first, then chicken soup and true confessions." She turned right at the next corner and we were on our way to Regions.

While we sat in the emergency room waiting for me to be examined, I asked Martha why she was home so early. She said the parties to the lawsuit had used the delayed starting time to settle the case without going to trial. "We were on the road home within an hour," she said. "Sara was missing her kids and, like I said, I was lonesome for Sherlock Holmes."

"But not for me?" I asked.

"I'll tell you how lonesome I was for you after I hear about the woman you were with and why you were with her."

"It was all in the line of duty. You'll hear all about it right after the chicken soup." At that point, a nurse named Jackie summoned me into a cubicle, where she removed the EMT's blood-stained bandage and told me how lucky I was that the bullet had grazed my shoulder blade and hadn't gone deeper. She swabbed on another layer of liquid fire and applied a fresh bandage.

"Check with your primary care physician in a couple of days," Nurse Jackie said. "We want to make sure that nasty thing doesn't get infected, don't we?"

"Yes, we do," I said. I wanted to tell her that I'd check with my doctor immediately after that heavy nether world frost I mentioned earlier, but I didn't have time for the discussion that such a statement would precipitate.

THE CHICKEN SOUP CAME OUT OF A CAN, but it warmed the belly and comforted the brain. Martha watched in silence while I emptied the bowl and polished off half a stack of saltines. It's amazing what running after a gun-toting brunette in red boots will do for your appetite. When I finished, I put the bowl on the floor for Sherlock's perusal. He sniffed the residue and walked away without giving it so much as one lick.

"I didn't think it was that bad," I said, watching the cat's rear end disappear into the living room.

"He only eats homemade leftovers," Martha said. "We're spoiling him."

"What do you mean we? There weren't any homemade leftovers in this apartment until you moved in."

"Maybe I'm spoiling both of you. Anyway, it's now storytelling time, and it had better not spoil my feelings of sympathy."

To make sure that it didn't, I recited almost verbatim what I'd written for the paper. I stuck unswervingly to the main story line, taking care not to wander off into such unimportant side bars as Kitty's dropped pantaloons, the pussycat paintings in her pubic curls, or poor Mitch's pulled off pants.

"Amazing," Martha said when I'd finished. "What you haven't told me is how you happened to be in that fancy hotel room with that woman."

I'd been working on an answer to that question while slurping my soup because I didn't want Martha to know about my original plan to lure Kitty into my—our—bedroom. "She talked about this fabulous room during dinner, and I thought it would be the perfect place to confront her about the boots," I said. "You know, quizzing her in private as opposed to maybe making a scene in the restaurant. So I asked her to take me up to see it."

"It never occurred to you that she might be the one who killed that Klondike Kate?"

"That had occurred to me. What hadn't was that she might be packing a gun. Her previous weapon of choice was a garrote."

"You never learn, do you? How many times have you been shot now?"

I counted on my fingers. "I think this makes three."

"Plus a stabbing, a solid whack on your thick skull and a couple of kicks down there," Martha said, pointing at my crotch.

"All in day's work."

"Oh, right. And how many other reporters at the *Daily Dispatch* have gotten themselves shot, stabbed and nearly emasculated?"

"Hey, I was hurt but I was never nearly emasculated."

"You're not answering my question."

"Okay, so maybe I'm not as careful as some people," I said. "But Al's been stabbed and whacked a couple of times, too."

"Which puts him in the same loony tunes league as you," Martha said. "And that reminds me, Al was coming out of this apartment when I got home. What was he doing here at that time of the night?"

Oops! I shouldn't have mentioned Al. My creative mind went into high gear. "He came here to give me the picture I showed to Kitty," I said. "And he stayed here waiting for me to call in case I needed him after I talked to Kitty. I did in fact call him right after the shooting, and he got to the hotel in time to take some shots of Angela bending over that Carlson character."

"That should make Don happy."

"I hope so. I'm going to be late into the office tomorrow, or I should say today, because I've been ordered to see Brownie first thing in the morning."

"Then we'd better put you to bed right now so you're bright-eyed and bushy-tailed for the interview," Martha said.

"I thought you'd never get to that," I said, wrapping my arms around her. This sent a streak of lightning through my right shoulder and I quickly lowered that arm.

"I see we're also putting you right to sleep," she said. "Come on, wounded warrior, it's almost two o'clock."

Chapter Twenty-Six

Seeing Red

NEXT MORNING MARTHA DROVE ME to the restaurant parking lot so I could retrieve my car. Holding the scraper in my left hand, I cleaned a thick layer of frost off all the windows, coaxed the engine to life and drove to the police station. On the way, I called Don O'Rourke on my cell phone and told him I'd be late because of a hot date with Detective Brown. Don said he was expecting a hot story as soon as I finished talking to Brownie. I agreed that we needed something hot because the temperature had dipped below zero again. Nine degrees below, to be exact.

I found something extremely hot in the police station. Its name was Detective Curtis Brown. I was ushered into his office by a sergeant and hadn't even said good morning when Brownie pointed to a straight-backed wooden chair and spat out the word, "Sit." His face, which was always tinted with red, glowed with a rosier than normal hue.

I sat and said, "Good morning."

"Good morning, my ass," Brownie said. "You've done it again, haven't you?"

"Done what again?" I asked.

"Turned a murder suspect loose."

"I wasn't sure she was a suspect until she pulled a gun on me."

"But you must have thought she might be or you wouldn't have had your tape recorder running."

"True."

"Did it ever occur to you to discuss your suspicions with me before going off on another one of your wild-ass goose chases?" Brownie asked.

"Actually, no," I said. "I was chasing a story, not a wild-ass goose. And I was going to pass on whatever I found out."

"How generous of you. And now, because all you ever think of is your goddamn story, we have an armed murder suspect on the run to God knows where."

"How far can she run? Last seen she was wearing nothing but pantaloons and a bra, which would seem to draw attention anywhere she stopped. Also, she left her purse in the hotel room so she doesn't have her money or her credit cards. When she runs out of gas, you've got her."

Brownie's face turned a deeper red. "Oh, it's that simple is it? Well, she must have had a Visa card stashed in her car because she bought gas with it at a self-service station at 1:15 a.m. today."

"Where'd she buy it?" I asked.

"No comment on that."

"Was she still wearing the bra and pantaloons?"

"How the hell would I know? I told you it was self-service. Nobody saw her."

"Must have been cold, pumping gas in her undies."

"I'll give her my sympathy the minute we bring her in. Which leads to my next question. Did she say anything to you that would give us a clue to where she might go?"

"All I know is that she came here from Madison, Wisconsin. She might go where she's got family."

"Makes sense," Brownie said. "We'll alert police in that area. Now how about giving me that tape you showed to Reilly?"

"Promise to give it back?"

"I promise to subpoena it and throw your ass in jail for concealing evidence if you don't hand it to me right this fucking minute."

Brownie's face had turned from scarlet to burgundy. Not wishing to be the cause of a cerebral hemorrhage, I fished the tape out of my coat pocket and handed it to him. As he put it on his desk, the redness began to fade.

"You can go now," he said.

"Thanks, but I've got a question for you," I said.

"You've got a hell of a nerve to even suggest that I answer a question."

"I'm a reporter, remember? I want to know if you've found out what kind of an affair Lee-Ann was carrying on with Carlson."

Brownie folded his arms across his chest and stared at me. I stared back. We held each other's gaze for a good thirty seconds before he sighed and said, "We haven't talked to him yet, but you'll probably wish you wrote for a tabloid instead of a family newspaper after you hear the story."

"Lee-Ann had a very active love life," I said. "I guess Kitty was right when she said she'd screw anything that wore pants."

"Including red ones, but she got more than a screwing from those."

"Will you be talking to Carlson today?"

"Probably. Depends on his condition. Now get the hell out of here." He waved toward the door and I accepted his gracious invitation.

"SHE HAD WHAT PAINTED WHERE?" This was Al's reaction to my description of Kitty Catalano's lower body art work. My follow story was in and we were eating ham-and-Swiss sandwiches in the *Daily Dispatch* lunchroom.

"You heard me," I said. "She had a pussy painted on her pussy. Like I told her, I envy the artist."

"God, I wish I'd been there to get a shot of that."

"Maybe she'll pose for you in the city jail."

"Oh, baby, I'd lock onto that."

"What if cameras were barred?"

"I could take pictures with a cell phone."

We finished lunch and I returned to my desk to find a message from Toni Erickson. I punched in the number. "I read in the paper that you got shot," she said when she heard my voice. "I was wondering if you're okay."

"The bullet just nicked my shoulder," I said. "I'm fine. Ted Carlson got hit worse than I did, but he's going to be okay, too." I'd checked with the hospital earlier and learned that his condition was "good."

"I was shocked when I read that Kitty told you she killed Lee-Ann and tried to kill me," Toni said. "I thought for sure that it was Ted."

"Why'd you think that?"

"I kind of suspected that he was the one who was banging Lee-Ann, so there was a good chance that he was the baby's father. And he always seemed to be running around in his old Vulcan costume whenever something awful happened."

"Carlson wasn't the only possible father," I said. "I figured it was Ed St. Claire when he took off."

"Oh, yeah, there were a lot of possible fathers," Toni said. "She let it be known around the office that she'd laid half the guys in last year's Vulcan Krewe."

"Maybe she was stretching things a bit. With the exception of St. Claire, the married guys in that Krewe told me they barely knew her. Now you're telling me that they knew her bare?"

"Like a reporter would get true confessions from a bunch of married men. I think the only thing she was stretching was their . . . well, you know what I mean."

"Whatever. Anyway, now you know who tried to strangle you."

"I still can't believe it. Kitty was like one of us, even if she never performed."

"Jealousy and hatred can cause people to do unbelievable things," I said. "I'm just glad you and Carlson are still alive."

"And you," Toni said. "You could have been killed, too."

I'd been trying not to think about that. The bullet had struck almost a shoulder's width from my head, and I have broad shoulders, but it was still too damn close. "Lucky for Ted and me she's a lousy shot," I said. "Thanks for the call."

"You're welcome," she said. "If I can ever do anything for you, let me know." The tone indicated that "anything" went beyond comforting me with mere words.

"I've got your phone number," I said. "Thanks again."

I sat for a moment, replaying the conversation. Toni had just painted quite a different picture of Lee-Ann than she had when I'd asked for a comment the day after the body was found. Back then, she had described Lee-Ann as "one of the sweetest people" she'd ever met. Now she was reporting that Lee-Ann had been carrying on a wildly promiscuous sex life and bragging about it. Come to think of it, Toni did say in the original interview that Lee-Ann liked to party. I guess you had to know Toni's definition of "party" to fully understand that statement.

Later that afternoon I also got calls of concern from Esperanza de LaTrille and Hillary Howard. Both indicated that they'd be available if I ever needed "anything at all." Apparently I'd made quite a hit with the Klondike Kate population. Good to know if Martha ever dumped me.

The last call of the day came from Detective Curtis Brown, who seemed to be in a much mellower mood. He had interviewed Ted Carlson, who had provided some details of his affair with the late Lee-Ann.

"He told us that he and Ms. Nordquist had been having a couple of nooners a week in her apartment," Brownie said. "Her little girl had afternoon kindergarten and Carlson would pop in as soon as the kid left for school. He said he gave Ms. Nordquist the usual bullshit about his wife not understanding him and she ate it up. He said that right after he told her he was thinking of leaving his wife, Ms. Nordquist announced that she was pregnant."

"What did he do when he heard that?" I asked.

"He said he tried to get her to have an abortion, but she refused," Brownie said. "He told us he was actually relieved when she got killed, but then he got scared when the pregnancy was discovered and we identified his DNA. Figured we'd see that as a motive, which we did."

"Well, he stayed true to form anyway. Angela told me she was hiding him because he said he loved her and was leaving his wife for her."

"His wife might take care of that problem by leaving him. We talked to her this morning and she didn't sound very sympathetic. Said she knew he'd been hanging around with the Klondike Kates and was getting something from somebody on the side. Mr. Carlson told us he had a thing for well-padded women, and I'd guess the wife don't weigh much over a hundred pounds. You didn't hear me say that when you write your next story, by the way."

In deference to Ted Carlson's oft-betrayed wife, I agreed to omit that juicy morsel from my report. I thanked Brownie, he gave me the standard "have a good day," and I went to work writing the next installment of the killing of Klondike Kate. As I finished the story, I wondered where Kitty Catalano was and what she might be wearing.

CHAPTER TWENTY-SEVEN

No Big Deal

MY QUESTIONS ABOUT KITTY were answered early Friday morning. I had just stepped out of the shower and was carefully patting the area around my bandaged shoulder with a towel when I heard the phone ring. Martha answered and yelled for me to come. "It's Don O'Rourke," she said, handing me the receiver.

"Don't tell me you've got another body laying out in the cold," I said.

"No, but the cops have got the person who left the previous body there," Don said. "Call your buddy Brown and get the story. He won't talk to anybody else."

Apparently Brownie had forgiven me for sending Kitty off to the races. I punched in his secret number and got the customary greeting. "Homicidebrown."

"*Dailydispatch*mitchell," I said. "I hear the nasty bounder is no longer bounding."

"Caught her in Denver, Colorado, last night," he said. "She was on her way to see a cousin who dances in a strip club out there."

"So how'd they catch her?"

"A Denver cop stopped her because one headlight was out."

"No shit?" I said.

"No shit," he said. "Why do you sound so surprised?"

"I told her that she should get that headlight fixed just a couple of hours before she shot me. She said it was no big deal."

"It was a big enough deal for the Denver cop. When he asked for her license, she said she'd left it home. He thought it was odd that she wasn't wearing a jacket over her short-sleeved blouse, and then he noticed that she had a blanket wrapped around her lap, which he also thought was kind of strange. When he went back to his squad car to call in for a check on her Minnesota plates, she started to drive away. He'd already called for backup and she hit the second squad head-on when she turned the wrong way on a one-way street. Busted the other headlight along with the grill and radiator on her nice, shiny Beemer."

Brownie went on to say that when they patted her down for a weapon, they discovered that Kitty was still wearing nothing but those red pantaloons under the blanket. Apparently she'd had the blouse and blanket in the car, but hadn't come up with a skirt or slacks. They arrested Kitty and took her to jail, where the matron made her remove her boots. They found her pistol, a .38 caliber Lady Derringer that she'd reloaded, in the right one.

"When are you bringing her back to St. Paul?" I asked.

"We're sending a team out on a flight this morning," Brownie said. "They'll bring her back as soon as all the legal crap is out of the way. Meanwhile, Denver is holding her on charges of operating a vehicle with defective equipment, driving the wrong way on a one-way street, reckless driving, driving without a license, damaging public property, carrying a concealed weapon and resisting arrest."

"All because she didn't get her headlight fixed."

"She could have hid out there for a long time if she'd got to her cousin's place and kept a low profile. If you're gonna kill somebody, it's a good idea to keep your car up to snuff."

"Words to live by," I said.

"Have a good day, Mitch," Brownie said as he put down the phone.

It was snowing again, but I didn't care. I whisked a couple of inches of fluffy flakes off my car, holding the brush in my left hand,

and drove downtown with a happy heart. The cops had Kitty and I had the story.

Al was equally ecstatic.

"They stopped her for a headlight?" he said.

"That's what Brownie said."

"I thought she was brighter than that."

"It proves that even the most brilliant among us can be undone by one dim bulb."

We went through the photos Al had saved on a disk and found a good close-up of Kitty he'd taken at the Victory Ball before she changed into the Vulcan costume. He also gave Don the shot of the red-booted Vulcan, and Don put them together with my story of the Colorado capture.

Late that afternoon, I got another call from Brownie. When I answered, he was laughing, which I'd never heard him do. "Hey, Mitch, what I'm going to tell you is strictly off the record, but I know you'll love it," he said.

"What could be that good?" I asked.

"We got a report from the Denver PD about your red-booted honey. It seems that the matron got one hell of a surprise when she strip-searched her." He laughed again. I wished I had a tape running to record this once-in-a-lifetime sound.

"What was the big surprise?" I asked, although I knew the answer.

"It seems that Ms. Catalano has a very unusual body decoration. The matron said it was a first for her."

Still playing ignorant, I asked, "So what is this highly unusual décor?"

"Would you believe that she's got the face of a cat painted on the hair in her crotch? Can you imagine that?"

"No way!" I said. "That's unbelievable. Did Denver PD send you a picture?"

"Don't I wish," Brownie said with still another laugh. "All they sent us was the standard mug shot. We told them we'd rather have a mug shot of the cat, but they said the matron was protecting Ms. Catalano's privacy."

"Too bad. It would be fun to run that picture in our weekly feature on pets that need a home."

"This pet's gonna have a home for the rest of her life," Brownie said. "And don't you dare write anything about it or you'll never get another call from me. Have a good day, Mitch."

He knew damn well there was no way I could write about Kitty's decorated anatomy in the *Daily Dispatch*. I put the phone down and went to tell Al. We agreed that we'd have more fun working for a tabloid.

CHAPTER TWENTY-EIGHT

Pleas and Pleasures

KITTY CATALANO WAS BROUGHT BACK to St. Paul the following Monday and her arraignment was set for 8:00 a.m. on Tuesday. Al and I arrived early and were up front in the biggest crowd of reporters and photographers I'd ever seen in the Twin Cities. The spectacular nature of the case drew representatives from all over the Midwest, plus a reporter/photographer team from Denver where Kitty had been caught.

Looking around the courtroom, I also saw all the Klondike Kates we'd met. Seated near them were George Griswold, the recently-unmasked Vulcanus Rex, and three men who I assumed were members of his Krewe.

Kitty was brought into the courtroom handcuffed and shackled, with a sheriff's deputy on either side. She was dressed in the standard orange jumpsuit issued to prisoners at the city jail, and her dark hair hung straight down in back, creating a Halloween-like contrast. Her face was pale and her eyes were lifeless until she came within ten feet of me. Suddenly her complexion reddened and her green eyes flashed as she mouthed the words, *Fuck you*. I smiled benignly and blew her a kiss.

The deputies turned her away from me to face the bench, and Trish Valentine, who was broadcasting live beside me, poked me in the ribs. "What was that all about?" she whispered.

"I guess she's a wee bit angry with me for turning her in," I said.

"It looked like pure hatred to me."

"There's no love lost, I'm sure."

The arraignment went as expected. Kitty replied, "Not guilty," to each charge when the judge asked for a plea, and he ordered that she be held without bail. Her attorney didn't bother to argue the no-bail order, apparently figuring it would be a waste of time.

When the judge rapped the gavel, the deputies turned Kitty around so that our eyes met again.

"I told you to get that light replaced," I said.

"I wish I'd put your lights out," she said. The deputies scowled at me and hustled Kitty away.

"I got that," Trish's cameraman said. "I got the whole exchange."

"Great," Trish said. "You'll be on our next newscast, Mitch."

"My fifteen seconds of fame," I said.

"Did you really tell her to get that light replaced?" Martha asked as we sat propped up in bed watching the 10:00 p.m. news.

"I did," I said. "And she said it was no big deal."

"I guess that wraps up the story, except I have one more question for you."

"What's that?" I'd been thinking I was home free.

"All the reports say that Kitty was wearing only boots, pantaloons and a bra when she ran from the hotel," Martha said. "Care to explain what happened to her clothing while you were with her in that room?"

Actually, I didn't care to do that, but I seemed to have no choice. The explanation flowed so quickly and smoothly that I surprised myself. "She was a little tipsy from the wine she had with dinner, and she decided she wanted to take a dip in the Jacuzzi," I said. "She started to get undressed while I was in the bathroom, but I was able to stop her after she'd taken off her blouse and skirt."

"A beautiful young woman was removing her clothing in front of you, and you stopped her?" Martha's eyebrows were an inch higher than normal.

"I swear it on a stack of style books," I said. "I stopped her by showing her the picture. I guess I should have let her strip all the way, including the boots. That way I'd have seen the gun before she aimed it at me."

"This gorgeous woman was getting undressed, and you were not?"

"I had my clothes on. Ask Al if I didn't. Ask the cops."

The eyebrows returned to their natural resting place. "Okay, I won't check out your references. Al's not a reliable source and you had time to get dressed before the cops arrived, so let's just forget about it. Tell me how your shoulder is feeling."

"Not bad." I pressed against the bandage with my left hand and felt only a nominal twinge. "I think it's healed enough for us to resume our pursuit of Swami Sumi's 101 positions."

Martha picked the Swami's book off her nightstand and opened it to the long-awaited Position Number 63.

"So, what do we do?" I asked.

"The first step is 'remove all clothing,' which we've already done," she said.

"Then what?"

Martha read, "'The lovers sit facing each other in the lotus position, looking deeply into each other's eyes.'"

We both assumed that position, although I had some difficulty persuading my knees to bend far enough to make it official. The disturbance woke Sherlock Holmes, who'd been sleeping at the bottom corner on Martha's side of the bed. He looked at us, decided we weren't going to settle down any time soon, jumped off the bed and walked out to the living room to claim his favorite corner of the sofa.

After about forty seconds in the lotus position, I could feel my right calf beginning to tighten. "How long do we do this?" I asked.

"It says that 'when the lovers feel compelled, they slowly slide toward each other, remaining in the lotus position, using their hands to propel themselves forward until they meet in the middle of the platform,'" Martha said.

"How slowly?"

"Too slowly." She flung the book away. "I feel compelled."

The End